This fictional story's origin is purely that of the writer's imagination. Therefore, any and/or resemblance of actual people to these characters, themes, and/or plots are entirely coincidental and should be regarded as such.

MAKTUB Trust Group

Presents

Men Are Not The Problem

Luna Charles

Table of Contents

Part I

(It is better to have loved and lost . . .)

There is no such thing as truth in love
Only the desire for honesty...

-       *Artamist*

It is better to have loved and lost,
they say.
Than never to have loved at all
You have to fall to get up, they say
So, you can learn how to stand tall
Life is full of pain and woes
Dreams are often full of foes
Time stands still, for no - one knows...
So, while you live, breathe, and see
Take the good and the bad in their
entirety

-- Luna Charles

Chapter I

When I was just a little girl...

I knew being in a house where I was no longer welcomed was my own damn fault. Michael liked things to end ultimately when he was done with them. Cut all ties, erase all numbers, and remove all photos that might bring back any memories. I knew this because, at twenty-two, he neither had a single photograph of one of his past girlfriends nor did he mention them. Those relationships had never existed with him, and he just wanted me to disappear in the same fashion. Since he was done with me. However, I could not, not this time. It was not like a year ago when he up and left me in our twelve hundred square feet apartment on Polk Street that I could not afford so he could move back to Sarasota.

"Miami is not doing anything for me," he had said. "I love you, but I have to go."

And go he did, but then things had been different. Finally, I lived close to my family and could move into an affordable studio without significant undertakings. The already furnished, one bedroom, one bath with the two-range electric burner in the kitchenette had been perfect for a newly single woman, and even though the queen size waterbed could be uncomfortable at times, it had served its purpose, and I had been happy.

Then, three months after Michael left, he begged me to take him back. I guess I was the exception and could not be as quickly forgotten as his previous girlfriends. Still, I should have known better than to listen to him, much less move to Sarasota to be with him. However, I had wanted so bad to make this relationship work, to prove that not all relationships I was a part of were doomed for failure. How wrong I had been. I had no choice but to accept accountability for knowingly placing myself in this situation. The beginning of any real change in someone's life starts when you take responsibility for your actions and circumstances. Yet, accepting fault for a failed relationship is hard, even for me, who should have been a pro at detecting bullshit from a mile away by this time.

So, I sat in the living room of our third-floor apartment, exhausted from the constant mind chatter and self-deprecation. My chest tightened with every step Michael took on the plush cream carpet as he paced back and forth in front of the large screen TV. The constant movement of his body across my vision echoed in my mind. Causing my breath to come in short and fast. I felt as if I would start hyperventilating. Placing my palm flat against my chest, I forced myself to breathe slower while silently telling myself to relax. This was not the time to show weakness. If I showed the slightest hint of frailty, he would pounce on the opportunity to prove how much I deserved this treatment.

I closed my eyes so I could mentally block him out. Flashes of the past played in the hidden chambers of my eyes like a movie reel. Heartache, betrayal, pain, and death, all those memories were locked in my mind forever. How hard I had tried to run and hide from them, but now I could not. This burden weighed on me heavily as I settled there that morning, listening to Michael's ridiculous reaction to the news of me losing my job, something that any loving person should have understood, but not him.

Leaning back on the black leather couch, eyes closed. I let Michael's words fade from my conscious mind and into the past.

It was the summer of my sixteenth birthday. I was sitting on my bed, exhausted from crying. My nose was running, and my head hurt. Judging by the brightness of the white curtain, it was afternoon already, but I had spent most of the early morning hours breaking up with my boyfriend. I did not want to do it, but I had to. The racial tension between his non-English-speaking Costa Rican mother and I had become the center point of our relationship, and I could not take him fighting with her to keep being with me anymore. I knew how much I wanted a loving relationship with my mother, so turning their relationship sour was just not something I could deal with.

Usually, my uncle would have barged in to tell me to stop all the dramatic whimpering and grow up. At twenty years old, he lived with us and was more like an older brother. However, he had gone with friends to God knows where. So instead, my little brothers entered my room without regard for my privacy. Michelle and Pierre had hung out around the house. However, with the sun shining and the wind blowing. Plus, the school was out for the boys. So, they were restless to go outside and play.

I looked from one dark brown face to the other, not wanting to go but finding no credible excuse. My youngest sister, Jennifer, slept with my mother in her room, which took away any reason I could have given for being unable to take them outside. Wanting to stay inside the house and mope because of heartbreak was not an excuse a six and twelve-year-old cared about. In addition, I knew if I ignored them, they would go by themselves, and it would be my ass for leaving them without supervision. I sighed, resigning myself to my older sister's duties.

Dressed in my white sports bra and shorts, which I had slept in, I told them to grab their stuff as I held my light and dark grey colored Nike skates from inside the bedroom closet and headed for the bathroom to brush my teeth. Within minutes, we were on our way around the block.

I wondered what they were up to while passing Lenard and Lee's house while trailing my brothers. I traced their chain-linked fence with the palm of my hand, using it in some places to propel me forward. The coconut trees on either side of the walkway that led to their front door swayed back and forth in the tropical summer wind as the large green fruit bounced off each other, making a thumping sound. Through the shut front door, I could hear the black Lab puppy barking, probably chasing one of the eight cats their aunt owned.

Looking away from the house, I noticed my brothers were more than a bit ahead of me. Speeding up, I followed them past the stop sign in the corner that marked the end of our block. Cherry hedges began where the fence ended, and a giant avocado tree sprung up in the center of the next backyard. Dead fruit lay scattered around the gray trunk; bugs gathered to feast on the rotting flesh. I continued moving forward behind Michelle, smiling at how his short legs paddled twice as fast to keep up with his older brother.

Dodging underneath some low-hanging branches in my path, I noticed how the sun reflected on the leaves on the ground. The day was too beautiful for me to be in such a despairing mood, yet I kept scolding myself as I moved to the beige house with white trim that sat diagonally behind Lee's house. I could see the yard and the side of the house but not the whole thing. Not until I moved forward on the sidewalk. The grass had turned the color of wheat. And had taken over the walkway in some places from a lack of care. I slowed down to keep from falling on the skates while trying to keep an eye on my brothers. They, of course, moved over the dangerous ground at full speed on the two BMXs leaving me behind again.

The smooth cement was interrupted every couple of feet from where the slab had been poured. I moved cautiously forward. Eyes on the ground more than straight ahead are probably why I almost ran into the side of the orange and white moving van parked in the way.

The giant U-Haul seemed to have appeared out of nowhere. I could not see anything from the front or the back of it. Furthermore, what was worst was I could not see any signs of my brothers. Fright overtook my apprehension about falling. I hurried around the rear and only briefly saw the massive layout of furnishings inside the parked truck. Momentarily, I wondered whose things they were as I rushed to find the two masters of mischief.

Once I came to the front of the house, I saw their bikes on the front lawn and them speaking to a youngster. He looked about the same age as Pierre but was slightly heavier and darker. He looked up at me expectantly. I just waved and moved away from the small group. Michelle stood a few inches away from them, fiddling with his pants pocket as the two older boys became acquainted. Then, deciding not to pound my siblings into mush for worrying me in front of the new kid, I sat down on the dead lawn a few feet away.

I thought this house being occupied again would be a load off my mother's mind. However, the house had remained empty for months since the last family moved out, and mom had started to get worried it might become an attraction for vandals and delinquents, warning me once, "Empty houses are just a calling card for bad children to act worse."

I knew the truth of my mother's statement from experience, from before I came to this country from Haiti and the many houses my younger sister and I would play in. My grandmother would often scream our name thinking we were lost when playing hide and seek, having tea parties, or breaking windows in a local abandoned house. Maggie, my now fifteen-year-old sister whom my grandmother had treated like my twin because we were only eleven months. Apart was my shadow when it came to causing trouble.

Moreover, she was always treated as a co-conspirator when my grandmother dished out punishment for not answering her screams. I missed her and wondered what she was doing to us. Homeland? Perhaps she was working, selling vegetables in the market to make money, or even cooking. But whatever she was doing in Haiti, I knew she was not enjoying an afternoon of leisure.

I sat on the front lawn of the newly inhabited house for a few minutes, basking in the warmth of the South Florida daylight, fidgeting with my bright green and black kneepads, waiting for my brothers to finish their conversation with their new friend. All the while staring at the house across the street. Wishing that my friend who lived there was not on vacation with her parents in Nicaragua.

As I leaned back with my hands resting on the grass to either side, a shadow came from behind and blocked the incredible warmth I had enjoyed. The boys went quiet, and all sound seemed to fade at that moment. Bending my neck backward to look up, I saw a man peering down at me from what seemed like miles above my line of sight. Dark jeans were all I could make out.

I moved my head back and forth, trying to get a better look at him, but the light was at his back, which meant whoever he was, he had a clear view of me while I only saw a shadow haloed by the shine. I sat for a minute, waiting for him to move, as he should have done or at least said something. However, he just stayed there looking down at me, unmoving. Feeling a little nervous, I turned around. Bending over on my hands and knees, I tried to get up as steady as I could with the skates on.

Quickly, his hand gripped my right wrist, helping me up. The grip was firm but not painful. Even so, I still flinched from the contact. Then, advising myself to relax. Nothing wrong could happen to me here, not this close to my mother. I finished standing up, reaching my full height of five feet seven inches plus the extra inches the skates added.

I barely reached his chin. He was even taller than I had assumed while on the ground. His beard's dark mat of hair would have touched my forehead if I had stood close to him. I gazed up, saw him staring down at me, and smiled. Two white rows of teeth glaring down at me from a quiet stranger caused my stomach to twist into an uneasy knot.

For one, the smile seemed to hide

something menacing behind it, and two, he still held on to my arm, though it was apparent he did not need to anymore. Lowering my gaze to the ground as I had been taught to do when speaking to an adult, I said,

"Thank you, sir. I'm okay now."

Trying to sound brave and respectful as I waited for him to take the cue and release me. But, instead, I could still feel him gazing down at me, smiling, unmoving, and mute. A chill went down my back. I gently but firmly tried to twist my arm out of his grasp.

I wondered if he could speak English or if I had done something wrong for him to hold on to me like this. Every stranger danger after school special that I had ever seen ran across my mind, and every threatening speech my mother had ever dictated to me regarding how men were, echoed in my head. I stood there, terrified of what was to come. Hours it seemed, I waited for my fate.

"Dad."

My head snapped to the left in the

direction of the word that broke the uncomfortable silence between us. It was the little boy who had been speaking to my brothers.

"Dad," he repeated, standing directly next to the man holding my arm, who stood there mute and apparently deaf.

"Daddy!" the boy finally yelled, breaking whatever spells the man seemed to be under.

"Mom wants you." He pointed to the open door.

My gaze followed the direction of his index finger. A very calm, petite woman stood in the doorway of the house in a black pair of pants and a floral shirt draped over her round body perfectly. She surveyed the scene as if there was nothing out of the ordinary going on in her front yard. The stranger looked up at her, and the smile quickly faded from his face. Then, without glancing, he released my arm and walked toward the house. The little boy followed without saying a word to my brothers.

Still stunned by the event, I waited until they all went into the house and closed the door before I moved. The instant the door clicked, the paralysis ended, and I quickly rushed my brothers back to their bikes and off the lawn. We were back on the sidewalk in mere seconds. I could feel the daylight still shining down on us, but the warmth seemed to have left its touch as I pushed my wheels hard against the ground, attempting to make each stride of the skates roll as far as they could away from that house. Looking from this house to the next, everything appeared to be expected, and nothing had changed. The whole incident had gone unnoticed by the neighbors, yet somehow, I felt wronged.

Silently, I followed my brothers around the block toward our home. As I approached our blue-on-blue house, I wondered how best to come to my mother about the episode or if I should say anything. Phrasing it the wrong way would only illicit her reproach. A pointed finger and an accusation that I was not careful enough in a world where everybody wanted to harm me. My mother's distrust of human beings was something she had inherited from my grandmother, who had been slowly force-feeding me since I came to the States.

Her screaming at me about something else she thinks I did wrong in life was not what I wanted right now, with my mind still racing and my heart pounding. We sped past our front door and around the coconut tree in the center of the circular driveway. Opening the gate for them. I stood aside as they paddled into the yard. They crossed the concrete sidewalk and onto the wooden deck into the back. Not even bothering to stand up his bike correctly. Pierre dropped it on the deck and ran inside the house through the back door. Michelle followed suit, leaving me to clean up after them, as usual.

I skated to Michelle's bike first, bending from the waist down to pick it up, coming back up, bike in hand, with my legs shaky on the skates. I moved toward the rear wall next to the back door as gingerly as possible on the slippery deck boards. I was almost to the wall when Lee jumped the fence into our yard, scaring me half to death. A small cry escaped me as I fell and landed on my ass on the wooden deck.

"Hahaha." He laughed, his long blond hair almost touching the ground at his feet.

All the blood in my body started heating up in anger. I waited for Lee to stop as I plopped down. He finally stood and saw me resting there, glaring at him through slanted eyes. Lee ran over to help me, grabbing me by the same wrist as the bearded man had. His gray-blue eyes were so full of merriment that he didn't even notice me flinching at his touch. I purposely fell back down in a heap on the floor so he would let go. Anger and pain overtook me, and I began to cry.

The younger of the two Bradley brothers, Lee was always more concerned with my feelings than Lenard. Quickly, the happiness in his eyes changed to concern. First, he sat across from me and apologized. Then, taking one of my legs in his hand, he began helping me remove my skates.

"It's not you. It's just everything," I stammered, tears running down my face.

"Oh, come on, it's not that bad. Tell me what happened." Lee said

"Well, this morning, I finally broke up with José," I said while whimpering.

"I just could take his mom and him fighting anymore. God, I loved him so much; he is such a good person. But I don't want him torn between her and me." I continued.

"Yeah, I told you that was what needed to be done. I know you don't believe it right now, but it will get better," Lee continued

"So, is that why you're so jumpy?" He asked while helping to remove my other skate.

"No, some family just moved into Natasha's old house, and the dad is a weird dude. I mean, weird. I was sitting on his lawn, and he approached me without saying a word and grabbed me."

We sat there and spoke about what happened with the strange new neighbor until the light from the sun began to fade. When my mom stuck her head out the door and gave Lee a look that would halt a charging bull in its steps, he had me laughing my head off for one reason or another. I had to go inside to cook dinner. My young mind forgot all my apprehension about telling my mother what had happened. Lee jumped over the fence and waved goodnight as he walked around his pool and into his back door.

Chapter II
Can Pierre come out to play…?

The next day, knocking on the front door caught my mother's attention. When she opened the door, the plump woman from the previous day stood outside with the boy my brothers had befriended, bringing back the event into my mind in bright, vivid colors. I remained quiet and watched them through the partially open door from my place on the couch.

The woman introduced herself as Mrs. Jean-Baptist and asked if it was all right for my brothers to come out to play with her son. They were new to the neighborhood, Pierre was her son Jack's only friend, and he had told Jack where he lived. Very cordially, my mother declined in Creole, our native tongue. She had noticed the accent in the woman's English as they spoke.

"He is not feeling well," she lied to

the woman.

"Maybe another time then," Mrs. Jean-Baptist answered as she walked away.

Gently/Gingerly, my mother closed the door, looked at all three of us watching her, and said nothing as she entered her bedroom. My mother, I knew, would not let the two boys become friends that quickly. She saw their friendship as a means of Mrs. Jean-Baptist becoming a part of her, and my mother did not like uninvited people in her life.

It had not always been that way. She had been fun and full of life once, not so long ago. However, since her last divorce, she purposefully isolated herself to prevent being hurt again, using our well-being as a façade for not letting anyone get close. Although she still participated in church and family gatherings, she was now primarily a social recluse. Whoever this woman was, my mother would make sure there was no hidden agenda before she ever extended her hand to her in even a greeting.

For the most part, my brothers did not care. They knew not to bring friends over and not to ask to go anywhere. But I was sixteen, and though I wasn't mad at her for being cautious after the life she had lived, I was weary of her constantly accusing me of trying to ruin her life by trying to have one of my own. Everything I did was wrong to her, and if I were to bring a friend over, I would spend the next week hearing about how that person would ruin my life.

In her world, there were no friends, only people who used people to get ahead. Everyone was regarded as a possible threat to her life, a danger only apparent to her and her third eye. The sixth sense she and my grandmother swore was the legacy of all women born into our line, the feeling that foretold us of impending danger through messages hidden in our dreams. This message, like all messages from fortunetellers. Had to be correctly interpreted by the dreamer for them to make any difference. I had never had any foretelling dreams, and if I had, I would not know where to start with the interpretation. However, my mother's dreams were a constant intrusion in my life.

Take two years ago, for instance. Mr. Louis, our neighbor to the left, had invited us to a pool party where he was to commemorate the graduation of his Big Brother Program students. I was utterly excited about it. There would be other kids my age I could make friends with, and it would be something to do outside my life's perpetual dullness. The house was literally right next door to us. I could have jumped over the fence in ten seconds flat. I begged my mom three ways to Sunday to convince her to let me go to the party, though I knew such a request was a long shot. Finally, she agreed. Her approval astonished me. I said,

"Thank you."

And ensured I was on my best behavior the whole week before the party, cleaning, cooking, and picking up after my brothers. Never mentioning the party again for fear that she would change her mind if she thought about it again. However, the night before the party, my grandmother called.

"I see children playing in the lake," she had said. "There is a shark, and Selene will get bitten and drown."

My mom stormed into my room. I lay on my bed with the television on and read a book. "You will not go to that party," she screamed.

Confused, I started pleading with her again. Finally, she said it was too dangerous and explained to me the dream.

"The dream doesn't make sense!" I screamed out of frustration. "We were going to be right next door. A shark in a pool, come on!"

However, nothing moved my mother once her mind was made up. Instead, she left my room sternly, warning me that if she found out I went over there, she would beat me. A threat I knew she would follow through on, so I cried myself to sleep out of disappointment.

The next day as I sat on the

wooden patio in the backyard, writing and listening to the merriment of children playing water games next door. I was the first to hear the girl screaming that her brother was not moving at the bottom of the pool. I was the first over the fence, helping them pull him out of the water and administering CPR I learned in school. I was also the first back home to change my wet clothing so my mother would not know I had been over there.

Later, I stood in the front yard with Lenard and told him what had happened. Unable to swim, the boy had used a plastic shark to carry him around the pool. Unfortunately, the device had become deflated during all the horseplay. And nobody saw his troubles until he was already at the bottom of the pool. He would be fine, but I was not. The similarities scared me mute. I never told my mom what had happened; I could not stand to hear, 'I told you so.' However, from then on, whenever she would credit her visions for preventing her from doing something foolish, I would listen with respect gained from that event.

So, when she came to us later that day and advised us that she would have to 'sleep on' the new neighbor to see her true intentions, we didn't say a word, just nodded our understanding, and went back to watching *Full House*.

The following day as I was cooking breakfast in the L-shaped kitchen, mother sat at the dining room table.

"I did not have any dreams last night." She informed us

My brother looked up at her, hopeful that no news was good news and that it was okay for him to befriend Jack.

"This does not mean I give you permission to be friends with that Jack," she continued, "I will light candles one more night on the subject, and we will see what happens tomorrow. Selene, feed your brothers and bring me my breakfast".

"Yes, mom."

"Sis, can I get some juice too?" Asked Michelle

"Of course, little brother," I replied

Taking the scrambled egg from the cast iron skillet from the stove, I separated it into three plates containing plantains for my mom and toast for my brothers. I placed them around the table. Then, walked to the fridge, poured a glass of orange juice for Michelle, put it next to him, and walked back into my room so they could eat.

Later that day, Mrs. Jean Baptist came knocking on the door. By now, I had started referring to her as Mrs. J. she came with Jack in tow seeking my brother to play. My mother quickly informed her again that Pierre was still not feeling good.

Two nights later, my mother still had no dreams to direct her about the Mrs. J situation, and my brother was driving her crazy with his pleading. Finally, reluctantly my mother accepted Mrs. Jean-Baptist's advances but warned that the boys would play at our house and his mother would pick him up before dark.

"It's only so I can keep an eye on her son and your little brother since they want to be friends. She seems okay, but something about her troubles me," she said later that day informed me.

I nodded my acceptance of her resolution but knew what she meant to say was that she would find out whatever was going on with Mrs. J. Therefore, when the first play date happened, and my mother asked Mrs. J to join her for some tea, I was not surprised. A week later, when she found me smiling at the pair sitting on the blue suede sofa in the living room, conversing about nothing and the boys nowhere in sight, she reprimanded me for being nosy and reminded me that she was still investigating Mrs. J true intentions.

I only nodded affirmingly and went about my business, knowing that her statement may have been confirmed initially. However, they were not anymore. I knew my mother had desperately needed a comrade since the divorce from my second stepfather. Although *my* mother had sworn, she would remain without any new companion for fear of what would happen if she took anyone else into her confidence. So, it was nice that at least she had someone to talk to, even if it had started out with her wanting to protect her beloved son.

Not allowed to go anywhere, I often sat on the front porch watching as the two women walked up and down the block trailing the nine-year-old boys. My mother, a head taller than Mrs. J, always looked regal, even though I knew she had the weight of the world on her shoulders. Her hands folded behind her back, shoulders straight, and her head forward. She walked with the ease of a military drill sergeant. But anyone who looked close enough could tell that the outer appearance was only forced bravado. Courage in the face of adversity, nerves that only showed a small part of her humanity when she broke down to remind me that I was the only one of her now five children whose father never cared to help take care of them. Who might this father be, though? Only God and she knew.

Mrs. J, however, had no force bravado. She walked absentmindedly, often distracted by what was going on internally. Her shoulders rounded down, head lowered, fingers constantly tugging at her clothes. Whatever was bothering her, she did not hide well. Unlike my mother, the round woman with an angelic face and long dark hair that she kept braided and pinned up with silver butterflies in her head was very passive and quiet. As if she'd had just accepted life for what it seemed to be. And did not care to go against it for any reason.

I believed her kind demeanor and easy nature served her well as an Intensive Care nurse for Jackson Memorial Hospital, a medical center she had chosen due to the high volume of Haitian patients that went there for help. In fact, that is where she and her husband met; he had been a refugee from Haiti's poverty and political corruption, who had been brought in by port authorities for medical screening to detect if any injuries existed from his boat trip here before he was sent back.

"It was not just his perfect dark skin and rugged good looks that caught my eyes," she admitted to my mom.

"No, it had been more than that. It was his words, the way he played the guitar. It was his smile and the way he spoke to me and held me that won me over. And I knew he was ten years younger than me, and I had only known him a few weeks, but I just knew we were meant for each other."

Therefore, two months later, she was signing papers for his release from the Guantanamo Bay detention center and getting married. Mrs. J spoke of it as a page out of a fairy tale. My mother, however, looked frightened beyond words. It was as if she saw a Mambo at the cemetery waking up a zombie. My mother knew Mrs. J had been conned, but instead of telling her new friend what she perceived, she remained quiet.

"That is the problem with women," my mother said after Mrs. J had left that day. "We are too gullible regarding who we trust with our hearts. We think just because a man says 'I love you,' he means it. Men will say anything to get what they want. Anything! If a man says I love you, you must always ask him why. Always, you understand?"

I said nothing; she did not expect me to say anything. But nevertheless, her words to me were a command. A declaration on how I should move forward in any romantic relationship, never trusting that the other person really loved me, only that they pretended to attain an item of value from me. Later, I would learn that no more accurate advice had ever been spoken.

The next day when Mrs. J came over, my mother went to work to find out the situation's truth. Because my mother, being my mother, was a little protective, like the Nazis were a little zealous. So, once she had accepted Mrs. J's companionship and heard about this faux fairy tale marriage, without hesitation, she became determined to know the facts within the exterior mirage that was their marriage.

Mrs. J's answers were always positive to my mother's inquiries, and she never informed me of any ill-treatment from him. But my mother took all her words at face value, never really believing it.

The first time he came over, my mother dealt with him at the distance of a leper, both verbally and physically. Why? I was not sure. Nevertheless, I knew from my first encounter with him that whatever my mother felt, she was right. In addition, my mother was particular. Her new friend was hiding something that might cause us harm. So, when Mr. J came over, sporadically at best, he was never invited inside our home, only entertained on the porch so that no evil would be willingly brought into our home. He would lean against the coconut tree in the center of the front yard as the women sat to chat, using his six-feet-four-inch stature to catch the bending coconut tree leaf as they swayed in the wind, pulling a sliver off sometimes to use as a toothpick.

Once he pulled one of those leaves down completely, peeling the stem from three leaves, he broke them into three equal parts. We all watched as he pulled a coil of sewing thread from his pocket and tied them into a six-point star. Then, asking me to go inside and retrieve a clear plastic bag from my mother's dry cleaning so he could make something for the boys to play with. I did this quickly, knowing what would come and wanting my brothers and Jack to witness it.

He separated one side of the bag from the other and laid it flat on the cemented front yard next to the tree. He placed the star on top and cut the plastic to match the wooden star's shape. Holding one point between his index and thumb, he bound the string around until it was tight. Without cutting it, he moved to the next point, then the next, until all six points were tied to the plastic and each other. Only then did he cut the string? With the leftover plastic, he pulled one long strip apart from it and made a tail, which he tied to the line of thread connected to one point.

Poking a small hole in the center, he threaded the string through, making sure not to tear it too large as he tied the coil of rope to the center and then to the two points on the opposite end of the tail. The string bow made a "V" on the fascia of the toy to help with balance while flying. Letting the thread unroll loose, he ran down the street until the kite took off into the afternoon blue sky. Walking back to our house, he handed my brother the thread to control.

My brother was delighted with the new toy. It was something that had not been done for him before. However, my mother looked at Mr. Jean-Baptist as if her stare could turn him into an ice sculpture on the front lawn. She knew he was trying his hardest to get on her good side, and she was not letting down her guard for him no matter how hard he tried

"Di merci," she said to Pierre without emotion. After they left, as always, she went to get the front hose and rinsed off the porch.

"You do this so that not even the residue of his wickedness will be left to produce you harm," she would tell me. What my mother did was not really anything out of the ordinary. It was just how things were in a household of my cultural background, where superstition reigned.

However, my mother did this so soon after they left that I wondered if he saw her washing the porch with cold water as he turned the corner. Then I realized she wanted him to see it so he would know she did not trust him and thought of him as evil. My mother, Maggie, was not the type of woman who would stay silent just to be pleasant when she did not like you. In fact, if you were the object of her dislike. She would make sure that you knew it through every action she took. So, I only nodded in resignation and continued with what I was doing.

Chapter III

one, one-thousand, two, one thousand...

Time went by, as is always the case, and everything became routine. Wake up, go to school, go home, cook, clean, take care of my baby sister, write as I silently watch my elders converse, take care of my little brothers, shower, sleep, wake up and do it all again. Life was monotonously depressing.

Then, six months into Mrs. J living there, a hurried knock came at our front door. I was up watching television in the living room, so I ran to the door to prevent whoever it was from waking up my mother, thinking it was a friend in trouble. Instead, she stood on the porch, half-carried by her young son. Blood oozed from her lower lip from a gash that had caused it to swell, bruises darker than her chocolate skin was all over her face, and beautiful hair lay in disarray, cascading over her shoulders. She stumbled into the foyer. I backed away, too scared to touch her, fearing I might cause her additional pain as she hobbled into the house. Jack looked like he had spent some time crying. Dried grey lines marked the spaces underneath his young eyes. Then, adrenaline overcoming fear, I sprinted for my mother. I stopped dead in my tracks and banged on her door with all my strength, knowing no matter what the reason was, I could not open her door without permission.

The sound, I'm sure, caused her to fall out of bed because I heard a thump. She opened the door to her bedroom, half awake, hair disheveled, and her face full of alarm from the commotion. I moved quickly out of the way, too scared to say anything, leaving her to see Mrs. J's state and come up with her own conclusions. She took one look at Mrs. Jean-Baptist and told me to lock the doors and call the police as she went for the machete in her closet, obviously having an understanding of the situation that I did not.

"No, don't do that!" she screamed

at us as we moved in unison in opposite directions.

The beaten woman dropped to her knees on the tiled living room floor and begged my mom not to interfere. Her knees hit the ground so hard that I was sure she felt the pain, but her fears overshadowed the injury.

It was her fault, she clarified.

"I started the argument, asking too many questions." She looked back at me and said, "You should never ask your husband too many questions that will only anger him. You should trust that whatever he does, he is doing it for the good of you both." She continued to state that although she was only forty-six, she was an "old woman" who could not satisfy her husband. Ten years of marriage had frustrated him with his inability to find good work.

"And since I pay all the bills, he feels like he is less of a man; he feels emasculated," she continued.

My mother told me to leave them as she picked her friend up from her knees and ushered her to the sofa.

Removing Jack, hanging to one end of his mother's dress for dear life as she kneeled in front of my mother as if she was a statue of the Virgin Mary and could forgive all sins. I turned and headed to my brothers' room, only to find they were watching the whole scene in the hall. Apparently, awakened by the commotion. But too scared to disturb anyone with their need for attention. They had just stood there waiting to be acknowledged. Half dragging Jack away from his mom, I ushered the three boys into my brothers' room. As I sat them down on the carpeted floor in front of the dresser holding the TV, I explained that everything would be okay. Unfortunately, my brothers' TV had no remote, so I positioned myself there pushing the channel down button, trying to find an age-appropriate program to have them, zombie, out so I could see what was happening outside.

When I came across a *Family Matters* re-run, Pierre asked me to leave it on since Steve Urkel was hilarious. So, I left them parked in front of the "boob tube" while I snuck back into the hall to mind business that was not my own and which would probably get me killed if my mother found out. Remaining out of sight, I sat across from my brothers' closed door with my back to the wall that contained the linen closet.

I listened to Mrs. J pour her heart out to my mother. At one point, I snuck into my room across from my brothers', got my notebook, returned to my previous position, and just sat there and wrote. My journals had become a sort of unorganized collection of miscellaneous quotes or observations, which I primarily obtained through pain and disappointment. I mostly wrote in them, hoping the world would make sense through the visual memory bank I maintained. However, the wisdom I sought still eluded me.

I leaned to my right and peeked at the older women. They sat next to each other on the sofa against the far wall. My mother turned to console her friend as she cried into the palm of her hands. She spoke about the countless affairs. Spread out over the ten years they had been married—the ones she knew about. The ones she feared uncovering and how she blamed herself for everything. My mom asked why she did not leave the "son of a bitch." Through a muffled sob, Mrs. J gave what I now call a lonely woman's quintessential excuse to stay in a bad relationship,

"Men will be men. You cannot expect them to be faithful to you. All you can hope for is that you will be the person they come home to at the end of the day. Moreover, I know he loves me and would never willingly hurt me. Things are just hard on him right now. That is the only reason he would ever hurt me. Deep down, he is a great guy."

I watched as my mother's jaw dropped. My mother would have been an inferno if fire could be seen in her eyes due to anger. Instead, she stared at Mrs. J as if her friend had somehow morphed into a Martian who had stayed hidden in her mist while slowly devouring her soul. My mother, it seemed, had suspected these truths all along but hoped that she had been wrong. Before my eyes, her demeanor went from sympathetic to apathetic. Then, standing up, she moved Mrs. J into her room, cleaned her up, and served her a late dinner. I waited until all this was done to crawl the five feet across the hall. And back into the room my baby sister and I shared. I read the statement that Mrs. J had made and that I had written repeatedly until I fell asleep, promising myself that it would never be me.

She and her son stayed with us until the next day when she thought it was time to return home. When she left, my mother instructed me not to let *that* woman back into her house.

"A person with such a weak character brings bad luck to your house," she explained. Nobody questioned her. Her words were law.

I knew why my mother called her weak. I was ten when my stepfather grabbed her by the throat and slammed her into the mirrored wall beside the bookshelf decorated with fondly collected garage sale knickknacks. He had intended to beat the truth out of her regarding where she had been, which made her come home past 6 P.M.

Instead, he ended up with a twenty-pound Native-American statue broken over his head. He later woke up sprawled on the house's front porch, my mother firmly pointing his chrome-plated .357 at his head. She explained to him that she knew of his mistress, that the only reason she had dealt with him still was for their kids, but now that he had disrespected her, his company was no longer needed. In addition, since he had another home to go to, he did not need to return to her house for anything. She threw the keys to his 1989 Dodge 1500 van at him, waited until he left, and blocked all the entrances to the home.

That night had been the last my brothers saw their dad inside our house, and that night was the last we saw Mrs. J inside our home. Each time she tried to visit afterward, my mom made an excuse not to entertain her. At times, when my mother saw her coming down the block. All the TVs were ordered to be turned off. We were to stay quiet and hidden as if she were a member of the Jehovah's Witnesses. All contact between my brothers and Jack was quickly severed.

Two months later, as we piled up on the couch in the Florida room to watch TV, we heard the gunshot, then the sirens. My brother, uncle, and I looked at each other, then ran to the backyard to see what had happened. The Bradleys' arrived in their backyard at the same time. The fence was tall and wooden; we saw nothing since we were caddy corner of the house. Lee and Lenard grabbed the top of the fence directly behind their yard and tried to jump over, but they failed. Not giving in, Lenard boosted his younger brother up to take a look. However, all they saw was the back of the house, which contained a couple of cops that warned them to get back to their side quickly before they got in trouble.

We all looked at each other from over the fence but said nothing as we walked back inside our house. Later that night, Mr. Bradley came knocking on our door as we stood in the hallway in front of our rooms, the same hall I had sat in to listen to Mrs. J defend her husband's actions to my mother. We heard that Mrs. Jean-Baptist's husband had beaten her to death with the lid of a toilet reservoir and then shot himself in the head. Jack, their son, had been away and spared from the massacre. The neighbor had come over to explain to my mother what all the commotion was about. So he concluded as he glanced toward our little group in the hall.

He heard that the son would be staying with family in central Florida. My mother stood at the door, blank of expression at hearing the news. She closed the front door a minute later and walked into the house. She gave us a stern look for eavesdropping and walked into her bedroom. She didn't cry or say anything to us about what had occurred.

My uncle had also been raised in the old ways. Went to his room without a word of guidance to us. So, we were left to learn from what had taken place and come to conclusions. My brothers, too young to fully grasp the information, were only upset that their new friend was gone forever. I tried to explain as best as I could that the world was full of bad people and sometimes bad things happened, but the news sickened me. Ghosts of the violent past that I had left in Port-au-Prince, Haiti, sprang up to pull me back into an old nightmare.

That night as my mother slept, I sneaked into the kitchen and quietly opened the door to the liquor cabinet inside the movable bar. Pouring some rum into a blue plastic cup, I silently closed the door behind me and moved to the fridge to add milk to the drink. Drinking rum at my age was not typical in my culture. Wine may be on special occasions, but not rum. However, what my mother did not know wouldn't hurt her, specifically me. And she didn't realize that Gloria, my Nicaraguan friend who lived across from Mrs. J and was in a grade higher than me, kept a bottle under her bed.

\She always gave me some when I went by there. She would not tell me how she got the bottle, but drinking always made me feel better when I was sad. Therefore, with that intention, I went into my room with the concoction. Sitting on the white tiled floor, I started to weep as my baby sister slept in her bed. I cried over Mrs. J's needless death and my mother's lack of emotion. I cried for all the suffering people endured and our lack of sympathy toward our fellow *man*. I cried just because in a situation like that, sometimes crying is the only thing that can be done, and the rum that I hoped would help had not.

I sat there, letting the waves of grief and pain crash within me. I wanted the comfort of my mother, the reassurance that only a parent could give to a suffering child, the security that only her touch could bring. However, I knew better than to seek her out. I was not welcomed and would never be. It was not that she specifically disliked me, per se. It is the norm for daughters and mothers to fight while mothers and sons are best friends.

No, it was more like I reminded her of a past she did not want to remember. A history I knew nothing about except for the rare moments she felt like inflicting accusations on me, full of clues to a puzzle I had not yet pieced together to make a complete picture. I had tried through the years to be on my mother's better side but learned the hard way that it was impossible. She could not love me as other mothers loved their daughters. Like a rape victim's spore, I was constantly reminded of what she believed was a horrendous mistake. Being a person of my age, I did not understand that.

Therefore, I tried to bribe my mother with more love and attention than other mothers received from their children. Breakfast in bed, meals when she came home from work, mowing the lawn, doing her hair, giving back massages, etc. My actions were useless, my love was denied, and my heart was empty. It was sad when you have never had the loving hug of any parent, maybe even a self-destructive thing.

Once when I was eleven, as I sat in the passenger side of her brown Dodge Minivan that she used as a taxi, I flat out asked her why she never said I love you to me as she did to my brothers. Between trips to the rear to take the passengers' luggage out, she replied, "Why would I say that to a person that did nothing worthy of my love?"

I died inside at those words because I had no answer. So, I stayed mute. My mind was racing to discover why my mother should love me, but I tossed each one that came forward, finding them inadequate. So, I spent the rest of the ride from the customer's house to our house in silence.

That day I changed. It was not apparent in any way. Coldness grew around my heart like icicles on a windowpane anytime she was near. Her words had wounded me in a way I could not deal with. Not then, not anymore. Mentally, I put distance between us, knowing that no matter how hard I tried, the loving attention I sought from her would never be mine. Therefore, I ignored her curses and only half-listened when she called me a whore or told me I would never amount to anything. She, I decided, was not going to love me. Therefore, I would not love her, and the emotion I wanted would have to be found elsewhere.

Nevertheless, her absence from me at a time like this made the coldness grow to a peak it had never reached before. For us to be only feet away but eons apart hurt like my heart had turned to solid ice and the frost was traveling down my veins.

She had not had to tell me anything when she saw us in the hall. I knew what she expected of me in such a situation. She expected me to be her version of strong. To be without emotions and to show no remorse in the face of such a tragedy. More accurately, to be her. I also knew if she were to walk in right now and find me in the midst of my sorrow. She would barrage me with words full of allegations. She would see my tears and believe I was silently blaming her for what happened.

Moreover, she would indeed be using both profanity and threats that stated. She was not to be held responsible for women who could not care for themselves. Not her. She would not be liable for anyone's burdens, not friends, family, or foes.

My mother was the strong one who had chosen a life of solitude versus staying married to an unfaithful husband with whom she had three kids. She had decided to divorce him when her youngest daughter was only eight months old instead of staying in a bad situation just to avoid people talking about the single mother with five kids. She did not care about how society looked at her or presumed she was unhappy just because she was unmarried. On the contrary, she loved showing people how wrong they were. Maybe that is why she ignored Mrs.

J's apparent need for support and left the woman she had been friends with to die due to stupidity.

It was not right, at least not in my thoughts.

Yet, I suspect she did this because she was trying to teach Mrs. J tough love. She wanted the woman to stand up for herself without needing a crutch like she had done.

Since I moved to the States at nine years old to live with her, she had pounded into my mind how bad my grandmother treated her. According to my mother, my grandmother was just a quarter inch short of being the most reprimanding Catholic, non-nun religious fanatic on this earth. My grandmother had tortured her verbally and mentally throughout childhood, thus hardening her against the world. Her evident and eternal dislike for my grandmother drove her and energized her forward toe to prove my grandmother wrong. Grandma had beaten my mother, a young girl, with a stick.

"You'll never amount to anything more than a whore," she had repeatedly told her.

However, I had lived six years with my grandma and had never experienced torture. If anything, she treated my sister, Maggie, and me like princesses, scrapping and saving any penny she found so we could have candy or ice cream once a week.

Yes, I understood the source of my mother's strength, but simultaneously, it was a loss to me.

Therefore, I sat there and cried. I cried for José, the one person I wished was there with whom I could share my feelings, but he was now gone from my life. I cried to allow myself to make sense of this tragedy. I cried to let the hurt out and allow myself to learn what mother wished for me. However, what she wanted of me seemed to come at such a great price that I did not know how much I could afford.

Yes, I would learn as my mother wanted me to. I would toughen my shell from the world but not shy away from those who were not as tough as I was. I would not harden myself to a point where my heart was impenetrable. In fact, as I placed myself there that day, getting increasingly intoxicated from the milk and rum, I made a somewhat conscious decision not to become like my mother in how she dealt with life and people. I would not be so strong if I became a granite pillar, empty of emotions toward humanity.

Chapter IV

Love is all we need...

Sympathy was what Mrs. J's situation needed, not apathy. Sympathy is an emotional response given freely out of love, love for yourself and your family, and love for one another as people who sometimes face demanding situations that we cannot handle alone. Mrs. J needed our sympathy. She needed somebody to be concerned about her since she obviously did not have the strength to be worried about herself. But nevertheless, my mother shunned her, maybe by doing so.

She thought her husband was the only love in the world for her. The cowardly, pathetic, and obviously sick man who needed to constantly beat her to feel important until her untimely demise.

As I became increasingly inebriated, tears blurred my vision while mucus n ran down my nose. I tried to stand but fell back, almost spilling my drink on my favorite jeans. My pain was turning into anger. How could such an educated woman end up so completely fooled? What happened to Mrs. J for her to believe she deserved that kind of treatment? Who had so wholly destroyed her outlook on life that she thought his beatings were a part of their love?

I knew what had happened to her had nothing to do with love. It had been the ultimate deception, a fraud, and a ruse. No matter what Mrs. Jean-Baptist thought or how sweet the words Mr. Jean-Baptist may have poured into her ears between beatings, he had never loved her. Moreover, her ever to believe he did, implied that she never knew what love was. Especially the most important love of all, the loved one, should have for herself. I was young and somewhat censored from the world, but at least my mother, in her own offbeat and distorted way, had taught me enough to know that I should never accept any man's mistreatment of me under the pretense that they loved me.

What was love, exactly?

I was not sure. Having been raised in a house where trust was given on an hour-by-hour basis. Love was a mystical subject to me, like trying to imagine what the wings of a dragon felt like.

However, when José and I first met, I was sure it would be easier to find a dragon and feel its wings than to trust he loved me. Although I was reproachful and aloof, he had been kind and patient. He had seen through my hardened exterior born from repeated disappointments and gave me everything he had to prove he would never hurt me.

Nevertheless, in the end, it had been I who hurt him.

Like those I read about in Shakespeare's plays, our love had crossed a crossroads, and being together was no longer practical. Though I wished I could have held him that night when my heart was so full of sorrow and grief, I knew that was an empty wish. José was where he needed to be, as I was meant to be there that night in a house full of people, yet completely alone. But no matter how sad I was, he was not there then. I was at least thankful I had him when I did. With the insight gained from my lost relationship, I understood that what happened to Mrs. J was not love but lust. A perversion of genuine emotion.

Yes, my first love experience had been short compared to a ten-year marriage, and of course, we were talking about that of an adolescent versus an adult. But, still, I think it made all the difference in regards to me differentiating emotional attachment due to somebody loving you versus somebody using you.

I believed love was the need to always make the person you were with happy, while that person, in turn, always wanted to make you happy. While lust only cared about how satisfied a person made it, it never genuinely cared about another person's happiness.

I had always had a way of seeing things differently than those around me. Maybe it was because of my hapless adolescence or the genetically integrated sixth sense. But whatever it was, my perception of people became even odder than it already had been. That night, I came to terms with the idea that maybe love was something everyone pursued but few ever recognized. Crawling across the bedroom floor, I retrieved my journal from under my metal-framed bed without incident. Then, lying down on my stomach, I began to write.

Love is a mystery,

Like the existence of men, the extinction of the dinosaurs, and the actual size of the universe, there are many theories about what love actually is, but no one can deem that any of them are correct because no one can really prove that they know what they're talking about. It's like the sunset over the ocean. Everybody knows it's beautiful, but what I feel when I look at the different shades of crimson melting into the blue of the sea will not be the same as a person sitting right next to me. Our expectations, ideals, and experiences all play a part in what it is for each of us and what exactly we get from it.

I had anticipated love to be a currency to get what you want from people. After all, that is what my mother had taught me. However, my understanding changed at the end of my first romantic tale. While it remained a mystery to me, I now knew that within the fold of that mystery were incredible secrets waiting to be discovered, happiness beyond reason, acceptance, gratitude, and fulfillment.

However, no matter how complicated or straightforward the world's idea of love is, I know love is not letting somebody beat you to death.

How could somebody think that bruises left after an argument were the markings of love? Is that why people believe the horrible things that happen on earth are parts of God's love?

Even at my age, I knew love should not cause you harm or pain. Yes, when you lose the person you loved, you feel pain, but that pain was caused by loss, not love. Moreover, sometimes people fight when in love, but that is anger, not love. I was only sixteen and knew at least that much about love. Yet, what I see seems to be different from anything else the women in my life are teaching me. Somehow, I knew that their outlooks were wrong.

And if their outlook on love was wrong, their perception of the world was false too.

It was as if a great veil had been lifted from my eyes. My mother was wrong. What she had said to me that night about loving me was wrong. She did not love me because of anything I had done or not done. It was simply because she did not know how to love. She had forgotten, like all adults did as they grew up, apparently giving up on love because they could not find the love they were looking for.

I fell asleep that night drunk, my journal falling out of my hand and landing on the floor beside me. Alcohol is a funny substance; it gives you the courage to say and think things you would never usually do, but it can also wipe your mind blank.

The next day the hungry cry of my sister woke me. I grabbed the journal and threw it under my bed, never looking at those pages again. Forgetting the lessons I had learned that night about never settling for someone who did not love you just because you had not yet found what you were looking for. And wondering why so many women went through life never finding the love they wanted even though they deserved it.

Chapter V

And then there was one...

"Damn, Selene, what the fuck am I supposed to do now?"

They were the first of many words I knew would be part of this verbal assault, which Michael had probably dictated to himself before speaking them aloud. I felt like I was watching one of his sales pitches. He practiced in the bathroom mirror in the mornings for potential new car buyers, except now I was the person he was trying to sell his point to.

I entered the living area as he ran his perfectly manicured fingers through his wheat-colored hair. His pinched nose and the frown on his tanned face caused the freckles to shift as he walked back and forth across the small room, making him look irritated.

Turning away from him and the pain his face caused me every time I saw it, I looked at the large window at the south end of the room. The early morning light was winning its battle against the windowpanes that fought to keep it out as it slipped through small slits across the room. I turned my head. It felt surreal. I had been happy here, though now that happiness seemed like a memory from a dream.

A scene from our one and only Key West vacation filled my mind.

Michael stood by the Florida Marriott suite window drinking coffee, looking down at me as I snuggled against the comforter on the king-size bed. A smile lit up his face as I opened my eyes as if I was the only thing he had missed on a perfect morning.

"You missed the sunrise," he said as he sat beside me and kissed my forehead.

Swallowing down hard, the pain threatened to choke me, and I blinked myself back into reality. *That was then. This is now*, I reminded myself.

Nowadays, there is no time to look at the sunrise or receive tender morning kisses. Instead, there was only this. This emptiness was full of pain. Remembrance and the end of the possibilities we had shared as a couple.

A Thursday morning in late May, not much past eight, we were home, an abnormality on its own. Usually, he would have been home alone on his day off, while I would have been at my boss's house making coffee and seeing which real estate deal was on his calendar. As his personal assistant, it was my job to make sure nothing got in the way of him acing every agreement. However, things were different now, and not for the better.

The pain must have radiated from me like Apollo's ray from the star. We gravitated around as I took a seat to endure Michael's exaggerated response to our present circumstances. I was sad, confused, and hurt. Yet, I held a tight grip on my emotional state, only allowing the rapid blinking back of my tears to reveal my inner distress. I was split in half, one part contemplating my honest belief that we were in love, the other listening to his overreaction.

Part one mulled over every detail inside me on how we had been so good together. First, he had been such an excellent friend sheltering me from the world when my ex-fiancé Daniel had cheated on me. Then courted me like something out of a movie, with the beautiful dinners, parties, and him standing up to his father for not believing an interracial relationship would work. I saw us as perfect for each other.

Now, this...

I let the thought fade to my subconscious and returned my full attention to the dismal situation at hand that was the center of my present life.

"Can you answer the question for me, please?" he continued, not expecting an answer, only wanting to make a hollow point by asking.

I was trying to figure out whether he would turn that lobster shade of red, which I had often seen people of a fairer tone transform into when upset. I had seen it happen once before with him. We were at a party earlier, and someone wanted me for more than one dance. Needless to say, Michael was infuriated at their boldness. However, when he didn't go from Pink to slightly beet red, it became apparent that he wasn't distraught, just annoyed that he would not get what he wanted. At least not as soon as he had hoped. Me out of his apartment ASAP. Since we were no longer together, he did not wish me to still live in his place.

I understood his point. However, I did not know how we had gotten to this point or why we were breaking up again. Here I was, two years older than he was, and it seemed like he was more in control of my life than I was. So, yes, I understood that since we were broken up, I should move out, yet I had not expected him to act like some asshole just because moving out took longer than expected.

How did I expect him to act? Like a human being with understanding. Like the person, I had fallen in love with, like a friend.

I guess I had expected everything else except the truth, and the truth is that I was beginning to realize the person I thought was not the real him.

I had known him for more than two years. And in that time, he had treated everyone except me with equal candor and sometimes disrespect, but all of it I took as him being a little rough around the edges. After all, he had not been raised how I had been raised. For example, lower your eyes when speaking to your elders, show restraint for the sake of others' feelings when talking to them, and treat everyone like you would like to be treated. Instead, he had been raised to believe he was the most important person in his life and that others who were not financially equal should be regarded with disdain. There is nothing wrong with self-confidence and believing that you are as, if not more important than, those around you for confidence's sake. However, Mike, Mike was narcissistic.

He had the sort of view about himself that allowed his mistakes to always, somehow, become calculated. He was never wrong. And I liked that, someone in charge of me. I had spent my whole life in control, being the big sister to everybody, always responsible, trying to portray the strong, steel-like daughter my mother wanted. Mike had been my escape from the norm. I did not have to overthink.

Although Michael and his dad were very different in many ways, when apologizing for his blunders, he took his cue from his father and bought me a present to show me how sorry he was versus actually apologizing.

Steven, Michael's dad, had been an abusive alcoholic who took out the aggression of his hard work by beating his mother and never showed Mike any genuine parental affection or discipline. He simply bought him all the latest toys for emotional compensation. Mike never raised a hand to me but simply bought me things to appease me when we fought.

Which we had done often. During those two years with him, we had broken up more times than in any other relationship I had been in.

I should have known better. I should have understood that this was not love. The night he left me stranded at work while he used my car to party with his sister should have been the end. Instead, however, I lied to myself, thinking what? I could change the outcome of a play I had seen a dozen times before, both through my eyes and the eyes of my best friend with her bad relationships.

I thought I was smarter than that. Yet I continued with it, knowing full well the only thing that had sustained his mother through the years spent in an emotionless union had been the drugs she had turned to cope with the family's style of *love. So,* I guess I thought I was different somehow.

"We were so good for each other," he had told me once. "I have never loved someone as much as I love you," he had said.

The first time we were in bed was surprising. I had few partners; none of my previous lovers was Caucasian. Therefore, I had not known what to expect, but wow. He almost made me forget about my ex-fiancé. Almost.

Then one night, as we were ordering drinks with our dinner at Chili's, the waiter mentioned that we had the same birthday. The look of surprise must have matched the one on his face. I remember all night thinking it must have been destiny or some silly crap.

I had been so blinded by what was in front of me. I did not listen to what was happening inside me. Moreover, Inside I was telling myself I should run, not walk away. Yet, I didn't listen, brushing off the warning bells in my head as my mother's psychological mind-molding against love began surfacing. So here I am in this mess and feeling like a child taking my father's oral dictation regarding what ills I had done.

I could feel every word from his mouth as if I was being made to endure Chinese water torture.

"Selene, you know this isn't fair! You were supposed to move 2 weeks ago." He shouted at me, causing me to flinch

The cherry-blond and brown hair extensions braided into my hair were tied up in a bun at the top of my head, and it felt heavy. I wanted it to end. I wanted to complete it. The beauty that was the new day was now turning dark for me.

I tried to find comfort in the calming scent of the Dial soap on my caramel skin from the shower I had taken less than an hour ago.

I looked down at my hands and frowned. Flexing my fingers, I noticed my skin's dry, graying texture. I needed lotion. Yet, I dared not get up in the middle of his lecture to retrieve any. Slightly reclining against the glass computer desk, my legs were in the lotus position like a monk in a Tibetan temple. I wondered how long he would go on like this, walking back and forth, hands gesturing in exasperation.

I mean, we had fought before, but nothing ever this passionate. At best, our previous fights could have been called cordial. Something would come up, and we would disagree. He would argue his point, I would argue mine, and we usually agreed to clash at the end and then move on. Maybe that is how I had expected the news of me losing my job to be received by him. Maybe with some disappointment, sympathy, and non-belief, but never rage and never this.

People can be very cruel to each other when they start believing the emotions between them and their partner are false, but certainly, no one ever anticipated this spew of venom echoing from his lips. I wondered if he knew how acidic his words were in my ears. Then, I asked if he cared. I decided he probably did not. He walked over to a nearby wall and slapped it, palms open.

"I know you want me back, and if this is a rouse to try and make things work between us, I'll tell you right now it's not. Going to work." He said he stared at me.

"When I first moved over here, I thought since my family was over here, I would be okay," he continued, "But then I got lonely and begged for you to come to join me, and though you fought it. I know you wanted to come. You were just too willing."

I said nothing, only absently playing with a hair braid that became loose from my hair tie, half-absent-mindedly. Half listened to Michael go on about how unfair life was to him. Half trying to be strong by tilting my face away from his and gazing toward the ceiling over his hairline so no tears would escape the walls of what I hoped was an iron will. Instead, he ran his fingers through his wave of blond hair again, sending a small cloud of dry gel falling in the wake of his back and forth pacing in front of the couch.

"Now, I have to wait another month for you to find another job and a place to live. I feel like you are trapping me. All because I was fucking lonely. This isn't fair to me," Michael said. He said, slapping the wall one more time.

The powdery white flakes from his hair gel caught the sun's light in its descent onto the carpet. I would have to vacuum that soon. When it suddenly hit me, I was unsure why that particular moment triggered a response. I do not know if it was the thought of me cleaning, cooking, and treating him like the damn man of the house, as my mother had always taught me. On the other hand, if it was something unknown that just snapped because, until that instant, my emotional response to him merely consisted of indifference and pent-up anger. I prided myself on being a strong woman who did not easily give in to an emotional outburst. Until that instant, I somehow managed to remain calm and stared at him as if he was one of the worst specimens of a human being. However, I had been growing more upset with his idiotic ranting -.

I should have laughed at each of his comments, knowing terribly well that response would have dumbfounded the bastard. And, in turn, made me feel a lot better. However, what you should do and what you end up doing are usually very different. Therefore, I cried into the palm of my dry, cracked hands. Not because his words had somehow morphed into invisible daggers and pierced the hard shell of my exterior. No, that was not it. I cried because I felt sorry for myself. Self-loathing hurt worse than any flesh-piercing dagger.

"Why can't you find your own place anyways? Go home, go back to Daniel, just go Selene." So, I sat there and listened to him go on with his ravings, unable to do anything ... but cry.

He was right, I thought. My circumstances were of my own doing. I had been consciously involved in every decision leading to this disheartening but ultimately avoidable condition. From the first kiss to this morning in bed, in the end, no matter what was said and done, I had made the wrong decision. I had put my trust in somebody who hurt me not only once or twice but countless times. I had picked him ...

Chapter VI

My mother told me there would be men like you...

Two hours ago, I had been in his arms, the strength of his biceps comforting me while I slept soundly in their embrace. Our hearts were beating as one when the first ray of the new day found its way through the vertical blinds to us. I closed my eyes tighter, trying to ignore the signs of the day that meant I would have to move from where I lay comfortably.

I had laid there nestled against him, falling prey to his kisses on my neck as I slept. His hot breath, mixed with the warmth from his chest, caressed my exposed neck until I stirred. Then, he wrapped his arm tighter around me, pulling my body closer against his, softly, slowly brushing his fingertips against my breasts, teasing my rather large nipples over the white cotton shirt that I so often wore to sleep until they were as taut as his penis against my buttocks.

We had already been broken up for three weeks. Yet, we still shared the same bed out of convenience, or maybe it was comfort. I was not sure anymore. I knew that morning there was nothing left between us, nothing. Nonetheless, through all the emotional anger that churned inside, I was like lava waiting to erupt. All the pain he had put me through in the last few weeks and all the tears that poured out of me unrepressed when he was not around to witness them—I let what I knew was happening move forward, never truly being able to deny him anything, not when he touched me the way he did. Besides, whether it was just lust for him or something else, my body's power over him was just as strong. Therefore, when we made love a couple of hours ago, through dreamless whispers and eyes shut tightly to keep the morning light out, I knew the day would eventually progress into something like this. I just chose to ignore reason.

I looked up from my hand to him as he continued about the unfairness of the situation when I finally remembered I could speak. Thus, I could defend myself from his verbal battering instead of just sitting there like a martyr, letting tears pour out of me.

"I'm sorry, Michael, things are not going as you had planned. After all, my life does revolve around you, doesn't it? I mean, why else would I have picked up all my shit and moved over here if it was not for making you happy. I mean, it is not as if I loved you and thought that you loved me too, and with that love would come a certain level of understanding. That would have been outrageous for me to think, right?" I yelled out at him. "Like me having to understand that after you had begged and pleaded with me to move over here, you suddenly need space and that this is not working for you anymore." I continued, "You are such a fucking selfish ass!"

"Just so you know, I would never consider staying here another moment longer than I have to. As soon as I get my check, I'm out of your fucking way," I spat at him through my tear-drenched vision while feverishly wiping my face on the sleeve of my Old Navy T-shirt.

Taking a deep breath, he rolled his shoulders to relieve stress. Then, he continued flexing his fingers in and out of a fist.

"Oh, and what will you do for money after that, huh? No matter how much Robert liked you as his assistant, the severance pay will not be more than a couple of thousand, which can only take care of you for a month, tops," he threw back at me.

I hated him for making that obvious point. But, of course, he was right, I thought bitterly as he finally stopped pacing and moved to sit down on the black leather sofa, caddy corner from me. I turned to face him straight on. His blue eyes stared at me, un-wavered by my emotional state. I wondered how he had somehow managed to look exhausted.

"Michael, I promise you don't need to worry about me. Don't stress your pretty little head over it," I said, finally getting a bit of self-control back.

"I would never ask you for anything. I've never had problems finding a job, but thanks for caring." He did nothing, not even blinking to indicate he had registered the sarcasm in my statement.

"You really don't care about how I feel right now, do you?" I asked a bit somberly.

"It's not that, babe. I have already told you ... I just need time to figure out what I want to do with my life, and I have to do it myself. Being in a relationship only makes people too comfortable to stop concentrating on what they should be doing. I'm only twenty-two, baby girl. This is ..."

"Bullshit, Michael. You know that is not what I mean. I was doing fine without you. I never needed you. After our last break up, you moved to Sarasota, and I stayed in Miami and moved on. I had a place, a great job with definite room for advancement, and dating a nice person who cared about me; I thought this thing between you and me was finally over.

"When bam, you had to walk right back into my life like some old Gloria Gaynor song, begging me to take you back. In addition, when I told you I had someone, you suddenly needed me, and you could not live without me. 'Oh, please, he could never make you as happy as I can't. How, if I left everything behind and moved back here with you, you promised I would never regret it. The worst part is I believed you. Against every bit of advice, everybody told me, I felt your insufferable ass.

"I left, moved to fucking Sarasota from Miami! For you! So, six months later, you can realize you need some space. You selfish son of a bitch! What about you ... What about me, you jerk! Do you ever think of anybody else besides you?" I screamed at him with more passion than I thought I had left in me.

I had risen to stand over him from my seat, so I talked down to him. My ears felt hot, and my fist balled into tight little weapons. I was so pissed off that I felt like I would hit him and keep hitting him until someone made me stop or I passed out from exhaustion. Finally, done with my outburst, I hovered there glaring at him, daring him to give me a reason to attack. Instead, he just sat there with his head bent down in defeat.

I stood there for a while, feeling the heat from my outburst boil inside me, waiting and wanting him to just say something. However, he didn't, so I sat down, drained.

"I'm sorry, baby girl," he whispered with what I believed was as much counterfeit emotion as he could muster.

I knew it was a lie, and I wanted to hate him. I wanted to hate him for every word that had ever come out of his mouth that I now decided had been lies. I wanted to make my body develop the ability to break out in hives every time I even thought about him, but I couldn't, and that realization only brought fresh tears to my eyes.

Damn him and his deceit. Did he believe I could not hear the insincerity in his pathetic attempt at sounding remorseful?

I wiped my face. Michael was not the remorseful type. Letting the heat cool out of my blood, I stared at him. The arched eyebrow, the tilted head, the sympathetic demeanor, and the remorse were not what I had heard in his apology.

It was a pity, empathy for my situation, and maybe some shame for him dealing with it. Suddenly I was sick. It hurt so bad to know that I was being pitied. I started to cry again, more challenging this time. I wish I could say that I was calling anew because I had not heard the undertone of pity in his words and was just still irate at him. However, my subconscious understood what his words truly meant: there was no more love, only empathy for living with someone who was now worthless to him.

I know what I wanted to tell myself. I wanted to say I was weeping because I hated Michael for pitying me, but I could not. So why bother even lie, even if the lie is small? I knew the real reason I was crying; I heard the truth rumble from somewhere deep within my soul before it came to bear fruit on the surface. It was because I felt like I deserved the pity.

In response to his faux apology, I looked down at him earnestly and told him to go fuck himself, followed by a word so severe that I dare not mention it. He said nothing more. He stood up from the sofa, walked around the glass coffee table past the Lazy Boy, and into the hall leading to the bathroom. I watched him; the confidence in his walk spoke volumes.

It had been that same walk and that same *phony* sincerity that had intrigued me into going out with him in the first place just four months after I had called off my engagement to Daniel. Funny how those things that make you fall in love with someone when you first meet and start dating are the same things that you start to hate about them when you break up. I heard the shower come on—I guess that meant our little discussion would have to wait until he had freshened up. I turned back to face the computer and caught a glimpse of myself in the screen's reflection. My face looked like I had spent a week without sleep. It was painful to look at, but I had to force myself to look, or I would never learn.

I moved to the couch, bending over to try to wipe my face of the last remaining wetness of my tears, but the water kept coming. So finally, I stood and walked to the window. Pulling the blinds open, I let the light flood in. The rays stretched over the room and enveloped me in their arms. I felt a soft breeze blow against my face, and I smiled at the warmth it carried into my being as my tears slowly abated.

I gazed at the lake across from the apartment on the third floor, green vegetation sprawled across my view, a momma duck being followed by half a dozen ducklings. No one was out there at this time; all ordinary people were at work living their everyday non-pathetic lives. Turning to look at the blue Dell desktop Michael's dad gave him for Christmas a year and a half ago, I wondered what I was doing here and why.

I mean, yeah, I knew I was in Sarasota because I had wanted to be with Michael, but why? Why would I have moved over here to try to make a relationship work that was not working when I was back on my side of the world?

Sitting down and staring at the screen, my mind went completely blank for a minute. Then, I heard myself whisper, "Omni a Vinci amour."

"Love conquers all," I repeated as if that was the answer to the question rumbling around in my head: Why had I moved over here and tried to make a dead relationship live?

Chapter VII

It could always be worse...

I went on roommates.com to see if there were any new people I could e-mail about possibly sharing an apartment. Mike was right; I could not afford to live alone and needed to get out of there quickly. Looking for a roommate online was not the safest thing, but it was the only thing I could think of.

Unfortunately, I heard him walk into the living room before I could finish my correspondence. I slowly exhaled, vowing to myself that I would hold my composure, tilting my head to look at him as he approached me from the rear. He was already dressed. A simple white cotton T-shirt that clung to his broad shoulders and narrow waist, boot cut, stone-washed blue jeans, and a pair of size eleven Nike Cortez. I had bought him everything he was wearing at one time or another.

My back arched as I held my breath when he entered, despite my mental warnings not to a few seconds ago. I watched him from the corner of my eye, at six feet tall, well-tanned, muscular with sky blue eyes that seemed always amused. He was the typical rough-and-tumble surfer type that you would find on MTV on one of those reality shows, and just like those shows, his looks may have been the only good thing about his persona.

Slowly, he slid around the Lazy Boy and sat back down into the seat he had just vacated half an hour ago. The gel in his hair made it look darker than the hay color. His eyes were focused on me. I could feel the heat of the stare trying to burn a hole into me. I turned around to look at him straight on instead of over my shoulder. My arms wrapped protectively over my chest.

We stayed there for a while, staring at each other, waiting to see who would speak first. I was listening to the ducks chattering coming from the pond out back.

"Come here, sit next to me." He motioned me over with his hand.

"Why Mike, why?" I whimpered.

"Please, so we can just talk for a minute."

"Look, whatever it is, you have to say I can hear it just fine from over here, and whatever it is, I probably don't want to hear it, or I've heard it before. Haven't we said everything that must be said throughout the past three weeks? Thanks, but no thanks." I turned back to the computer screen.

"Look, I already said I'm sorry. I just want to talk, okay?"

I turned back around and stared at him for a minute. His nose was slightly bent and never healing properly after he broke it in a fight a few years back, and deliciously pink lips. His eyes were so warm you wondered how anybody could deny him anything. I would slowly go insane if I did not learn to control how much I was still attracted to him.

Giving in to his request, I used my bare feet to propel the computer chair to

Michael's sofa. I stopped when I smelled the scent of the soap on his skin, realizing I was not ready for being this close to him. So, I moved back a bit. I would be as close to him as possible but not close enough to smell him.

"Why are you staying here?"

God-dammit was all I thought when that question was the first thing out of his mouth. It made me groan. He wasn't talking about the apartment. He was talking about Sarasota; I had been right in my inclinations that I had heard this before.

"First, it was me," he continued, "I mean, it was me that brought you here, and when we broke up—"

"Again. Because of you—" I intercepted and told myself to let it go.

"Yes, again, because of me. Then, your exciting job as Robert Andrew's personal assistant kept you here. But now that you've lost me and your job, why won't you return home?" He was trying to sound like my motives were beyond his understanding, that there was no reason to stay for a person who was so far from home and had nothing. Because, of course, he thought there was no me without him in my life. I should just give up and disappear now that he was done with me. However, he was wrong. I did not need him to be me, to be Selene, the incredible, beautiful, successful me. I just wanted him in my life, and maybe my reasons for being here were beyond his understanding, but I did not care.

In all actuality, we had had this conversation before. Michael had asked me this same question in different ways. However, unlike him, I would not rearrange my answer in the hope that making the words sound different would somehow change the recipient's overall acceptance of them. So, my answers were not going to change; I did not want to move back home. My reasoning seemed quite simple, though a bit unreasonable, I must admit. The simple fact was I would not go running home with my tail between my legs like a defeated dog because this relationship had failed again.

Moving to Sarasota was the first time I was this far away from Miami since I moved to this country more than a decade ago. I had left my apartment without my mother's knowledge for fear of what her verbal thrashing would be like. Although I lived alone and was twenty-four years old, I still feared what words would come out of my mother's mouth and how they would sting. In addition, although I had done it for all the wrong reasons, I could not bear to be told, "I told you so," by everyone that had told me so, which was almost everyone I knew in Miami.

No, I would not do it, I told myself. I was strong enough to survive this and more. Plus, it was not just because I was still in love with Michael. I had grown fond of this quiet, slightly redneck town. It only looked like a picturesque Americana settlement, but under the first layer of perfectly trimmed lawns and elderly retirees was a dark side that I had yet to uncover, which intrigued me. I thought of it as a big adventure, one that I could use the atmosphere to accomplish some writing that I had postponed. Besides, I did not know anybody here, which meant nobody really knew me, which was a perfect situation for someone who wanted to start their life over. Here I had no past, just the present and future. I could lose all the fear of disappointing people and concentrate on myself. So many mistakes I had made trying to make others happy.

My instincts have always subconsciously tried to keep me from making those mistakes, trying to keep me from places where maybe I did not actively know danger lay but inactively did. A flat tire here, stain on my clothes there, something would always happen as I ran out the door. Something that had to be attended to, even if it was just a whispered thought in my ears that told me to stay home, but I am human, therefore, stubborn. Thus, I never listened to my instincts; by the night's end, I was in more trouble than the party was worth. Anyway, Miami was not going anywhere soon.

"I don't want to move back home, Michael. And, I have no intentions to, so just deal with it and drop it," I told him, which was honest to God's truth *at the time*.

"Okay, but look, it would be best if you went home. You don't have anything here except my friends and me." He stopped and stared at me as if his gaze should somehow telekinetically transfer the message that his words were failing to convey. Stay away from my friends, was what he thought; they are my friends, not yours.

The thing about Michael is that I believed he really did care for me in a "hidden, too scared to show it, need to run from any emotional attachment" sort of way. He loved to love you when he needed you, but as soon as you might need him, he got scared shitless at the prospect of responsibility and ran for the hills. He was greedy, lustful, and envious; I may have been one or all of those things. But nevertheless, I wore my heart on my sleeve and cared for the people I was in a relationship with, and I did not just use them. Anyway, the jerk, at this point, was worried that I would stay here and take his friends from him.

"I'm not going to hang out with your friends—in case you forgot, I have no problem making my own. A verbal promise, which I knew, he was expecting and that I cared nothing about. "I'm not moving back home, so please, drop it! At any rate, why do you care as long as I am out of your way to *'find yourself?'*" He continued to gape at me. I did not mind the stare anymore. However, I was beginning to think his gaze had turned into a glare of annoyance.

"I'm not moving back home, so please, drop it! At any rate, why do you care as long as I am out of your way to *'find yourself?'* He continued to gawk at me. I did not mind the stare anymore. However, I was beginning to think his gaze had turned into a glare of annoyance.

"Fine, Selene, whatever you want." He rubbed the profile of his chin with the inside of his palm. As if to feel any stubble he had not caught with a razor earlier. Then, he shifted his gaze down as he asked, "Did you get your period yet?"

Shit! How could I have forgotten *that?* My period had been late for two months, and I had not overthought it. That is just the way my body was sometimes. My period just showed up sometimes, and other times it did not. However, sometimes when I was *late*, it meant I had decisions to make. Nevertheless, at that moment, I was praying that one of those decisions was not something I had to make. Damn, there was always icing for whatever fucked up cake I baked myself into, and the possibility of being pregnant while all this was going on served that purpose sweetly.

"No, I haven't ..." I pushed myself backward, putting more space between us. The chair rolled toward the desk but was not close enough for me to reach it. In addition, the apartment's floors were carpeted and hindered my movement.

"This is another conversation we've had. You would pick up a test for me when you got a chance. However, I understand you have been busy. You have had so much going on in your life, this relationship, work, and you starting over. So, it's okay. Just take your time. The test is not that important. We can just do it like they used to in the old days. Just wait nine months, and see if anything pops out."

My sarcasm had not been ignored this time. Michael's eyes shone for a few minutes with a light of pure anger. I pushed myself further away from him. Then, finally, he stood, and my breath caught in my lungs out of fear. Michael was not violent, but everyone had his or her breaking point. He looked down at me as he moved my chair to one side.

"I'm not going to do this with you, Selene."

He moved around to the front of the computer. I caught a whiff of his cologne mixed with the soap he had used as he bent over the keyboard. A flash of us intertwined in bed this morning flashed behind my eyelids. I gritted my teeth and took it. Good girl, I thought. I would not physically react to him while he was close enough to notice.

He typed his online bank address, account number, and password in the toolbar. His blue jean-clad ass pointed at my face as he checked his account balance. It was not a wrong view, even though I hated to admit it. Finally, satisfied with everything, he stood in front of me.

"I'll get one while I'm gone. I'll be back in two." He bent over to kiss me on the forehead, and I closed my eyes without thinking. He walked around and passed me like this little drama had never happened.

After he kissed me, my eyes stayed closed for a while; his cologne swallowed me, and memories of us in bed raced from behind my secure lids. I dared not open my eyes to watch him leave. Then, finally, I heard the door close behind him. Only then did I allow the flow of pent-up tears to begin their descent again? I wished crying did help me feel better and abate the sorrows of my heart.

"Father," I prayed silently, "help me stop loving him because I can't do it alone." Though I already knew my prayer would be fruitless, I held on to it with hope. This only made me human.

After all, people are people. Although dreams may change, time may fly, memories may lose clarity, and lessons may not be learned until it is too late, we still hope, pray, and wish that the bad things that happened in our lives did not. Moreover, when they do, we hope and pray that whatever is going on will somehow stop, rewind and give us a do-over. But, unfortunately, although we know by the time we pray, it is usually too late for any positive outcome to be reached for the present circumstance.

Still, we pray, hoping if we do not get cheerful ending out of it, at least we can get the strength to endure learning another life lesson that we might have already known but forgotten. It is a sad state of existence, doomed by faith or our desire to continue a never-changing wheel, trying to jump off but only repeating our mistakes. I have been here before. Everything felt so familiar as if I was having a bad case of déjà vu, and at this point, I could almost swear all my relationships had been with the same person. Sure, the ethnicities were different. The height, weight, dress style, and bed move were all extra. But nevertheless, ultimately, they were all the same person.

It was as if destiny had given me the same test repeatedly. Like any foolish, hard-headed child, I knew the pot was hot and kept touching it until an accident so harsh would leave me with a third-degree burn as a constant reminder not to feel it again. Then, still, blindly, I walked straightforwardly, hand unwavering, reaching for it and forgetting about the last burn.

That is what happened between Michael and me. One scar had not yet healed from my engagement disaster when I met him and forgot about the emotional roller coaster my heart was still dealing with. That I was not yet a whole person capable of love, but a shattered one that would have used anything as an adhesive to piece me back together. That is what lust is, a bond, something you use to section you back together. The only problem is it's like Elmer's glue, the strength only lasts for a short while, and when the strength finally gives up, it leaves a nasty mark.

Moreover, although I went from the lust that made me hot, watching the way his perfectly shaped ass filled out his Gap khakis, to being in love with the strength of his fingertips as they locked on to my shoulders, his biceps flexing as I rode him in the heat of passion. However, while I allowed myself to traverse certain boundaries I should not have, he never did. There is a thin line between love and hate and an even more delicate line between love and lust, but it's when you allow those lines to blur—that's when you end up in my present situation of yelling, crying, and praying. Lines blurring, lessons already learned, forgotten.

I moved from the chair to the couch and sat down, staring at nothing, letting the turmoil in my head swirl so fast it became nothingness. Oblivious to what was in the now. Instead, I chose to retreat into my past to find answers. To the questions that had begun to form in my head.

Questions like. How did I get here, and why?

Chapter VIII

In a land far, far away...

My grandmother was only 5'2" tall and maybe 90 pounds soaking wet, but when I was three years old, she appeared omnipotent to me, holding my sister and my hands as we watched our mother drive away down the red dirt road in the silver Honda. Little did I know it would be six years until I saw her again. That night my mother left, and my grandmother became matriarch in a household of four sons and two granddaughters without apparent means of supporting us. Being only three, I did not understand what was happening or know how things would change with my mother being gone.

My mother was an ambitious woman who never really liked how she was raised in a poor family. But who has ever enjoyed being poor? The second oldest of six children, she sometimes had to beg on the street for coins to take home and give to the family for food. Beautiful by genetics, she had many would-be suitors, like my grandmother, but unlike my grandmother, my mother only associated with those who could do more than just afford to take care of her.

They had to be able to care for the whole family, and she made sure when it came time for her to have her children, we would never be poor. However, she did not realize that we would never be rich. Instead, we were in limbo between the dominating social classes. You see, where I am from, there is no such social status as middle-class, so I cannot use that to adequately describe what we were financially.

You were either high on the economic status ladder or very low there. And where you were at any given time never had anything to do with how hard you worked, your education, or who your parents were. After all, my grandmother and 90% of the population worked hard and were still dirt poor. So, no, that was not the secret to success there. The secret to your monetary level in my country was determined by whom you knew or were "*involved*" with. If your present social group consisted of friends such as the newest political leaders, Generals, or presidents. Then you ate well, slept well, and were well taken care of.

However, if there was a coup d'état of whatever political party you were friends with at the time, you and your family went into hiding in an undisclosed location until the turmoil subsided or you were captured and tortured for the information you probably didn't have then killed in some horrific manner, comparable to being burnt alive in a truck fire. I've seen that happen to a person. The smell alone gave me nightmares until I was fifteen years old. Until this day, the scent of burning rubber makes me gag and causes a flash of the charred and melting body to pass behind my eyelids.

My mother knew all the risks when she got involved in the game of politics, yet she took them to keep us from having to beg. Thus, this was how we spent our early childhood years in a perpetual seesaw state of financial wealth.

My grandmother, a simple farm woman from the mountains, did not appreciate my mother's involvement in such dangerous games for monetary gain, especially with my sister and I being involved. Nevertheless, my mother had a taste for the best in life, making it a point to play the game. Until she met a Haitian-American who promised her riches unimagined in the States and left us behind to provide a better future for us.

My grandmother never wanted to play the games that would leave us sometimes poor, sometimes decadent, but usually, in fear, she simply reverted to living the only way she knew how poorly. Farming the land, growing what we could eat, and when we couldn't eat, we accompanied her to the market at the break of dawn to peddle our little hearts out so we could buy what we couldn't grow. My mother sent back money from the States, but that money was primarily used for shelter and clothing, and if there was any leftover, we went to school.

My uncles did what they could for work, but it was hard when you were a young man with no experience and minimal literacy. Literacy: To be literate, you would have to spend the money you could use for food. So, it was either starving for their education or remaining ignorant and living. Then, even when you could somehow hustle to make the extra money, you needed to be educated. You had to deal with an applicant for the same job that *knew someone.*

In those years, my country was in a constant state of civil war, the poor against the rich, the lighter complexion citizens against the darker-skinned ones, and brother against brother. As a result, although I was young, I lived in a state of perpetual emotional drift, like a waking dream, up one minute and down the next, but never knowing why. It was as if I felt I was missing my mother. Though I had now spent so much time not seeing her, I had forgotten all about her. And even though so many died in our cities' streets. I was never scared for my life.

Not till one day at school when some kid called me a white roach.

The sun was beaming, and the red clay dirt was dry and flaky, floating through the air in moisture-sucking clouds, leaving our skin and throat desperate for water. I was sitting under an almond tree with Maggie memorizing a poem we had to recite in class when I first heard it. White roach? How gross! I must have thought, having the image of the almost translucent bug flash in my head. The term was something the darker-skinned people called. The lighter-skinned people in Haiti were not liked because white roaches only lived in the deepest darkest shit holes and were far more disgusting than the dark roaches.

At first, I did not know he was talking about me. So, I only stopped and looked up to see who had said it. He stood about ten feet from us, pointing directly at me as he spoke. I did not know the kid, so I figured he could not be talking about me as he pointed his finger in my direction while commenting to his friends. I stared at him for a second, confused, almost deciding that I had heard him wrong. But he repeated it.

"Ravert !blanc!"

Before I knew it, my books were on the ground, and I ran full speed ahead in my pleated, blue plaid uniform dress. I am unsure whether strength or speed caused me to shove him to the ground since he was definitely more extensive than I was, but I did not care. All I knew was I would teach him not to call me such a disgusting thing. Tears ran down my face. Then, with my hands balled up in tight little fists, I pounded the crap out of him in a blind fury. I was so into the fight that I didn't even notice my sister kicking him beside us.

Finally, the nun that taught us came and took my sister and me by the ears away from the boy. But by then, the damage was done. He was dirty and bleeding. Yet, that did not stop him from calling me a white roach as I was dragged away. Back to the room where the class would be later held, I tried to explain to Sister François that it was his fault, that he had been taunting me, but she would not hear of it. All that came out of her was she would teach us proper manners.

When our youngest uncle, Emerson, got out of school and came for us, our knuckles were red and swollen from the hits we received from the meter stick.

When we got home, and I tried to explain to my grandmother what had happened, she advised me there was no need to. The neighbor had already told her, and I should have known better than to fight in a school she hardly had the money to send us to in the first place. But, instead, she looked furious, sitting at the small wooden table where we ate in the kitchen.

As she dragged us to the boy's house to apologize, she cautioned me. I had to be careful that, yes, I was different, but that was just something I would have to grow a thick skin about and deal with.

After she apologized profusely for the actions of her troublemaking granddaughters to the boy's mother, she took us home and taught us not to embarrass her anymore. We could not sit the whole night after that.

That night, as I lay on my stomach trying to sleep, I could not get the thought of being different out of my head. A white roach, the lowest of the insects.

I was never the same after that day, instead of finding nourishment and comfort in the people around me. And in the love of my country, when I looked around. I only saw the fear inside my neighbors' eyes. I felt like I was under a microscope, with everybody looking at me and my skin as if I did not belong. I became introverted.

Two years passed without me ever making any new friends, much less getting into a fight. I stayed home and close to my family because, at least there, I knew no harm would come to me. Then, finally, in the winter of my ninth birthday. My mother sent for me after over seven years of living in poverty and fear without her.

My trip to the States was more like an abduction. Then a little girl being sent to live with her mom. So, first of all, no one told me anything for fear that I would tell somebody and end up kidnapped, which was very likely.

Everything happened so fast that I could not believe how precise the details were still in my head.

I was awakened in the dead of night. Someone was sitting there pulling on my toes. Startled by the unwanted attention and slightly annoyed because I had a wonderful dream of all different color paints melting together to form one brilliant new hue, I desperately wanted to know what it was. I tried several times to struggle out of the death grip the person had on my toes, to no avail. Finally, grunting, admitting defeat, I sat up, rubbing my eyes, perturbed to face my adversary. A single candle on the nightstand lit the room; the glow barely penetrated the opaque darkness.

My uncle nicknamed *Tit Frè (little brother) for* being my mom's first younger brother. Though he was the oldest male from my grandmother, he was there kneeling by the foot of the bed, motioning for me to get dressed in something more than my sleeping shirt and come with him. He was a tall, dark man with sorrowful eyes and a thick handlebar mustache; he was not one to be argued with. He firmly believed in the rule that dictated that children should be seen and not heard, so I didn't ask any questions and just slid out of bed to get dressed.

I did this with all the clumsiness of a half-awake nine-year-old girl. One of that night's greatest mysteries is how my eight-year-old little sister continued sleeping undisturbed throughout the event. Even though we shared one bed, I went out of my way to wake her. Nevertheless, she remained there sleeping. The only way you knew she was even there was because of the small round shape her form made sleeping in the fetal position underneath the bed cover. So, I never got a chance to say goodbye to her.

I was given a worn-out brown suitcase that weighed almost nothing. My grandmother hugged me and told me to sit on the passenger side of my uncle's late model, Datsun. My grandmother and her third eldest child spoke for a few moments, out of hearing range, then she came to the car, kissed me once more, and said, *"Di momou, nou preyay pouli shak jou."* She closed the car door for me and walked away without looking back.

I sat there, hugging myself, too afraid to cry. Worried that if my tears began to flow, it would give life to my fears and keep my long-held dreams from coming true. 'Tell your mom we pray for her every day,' my grandmother had said. Then, finally, my uncle got behind the steering wheel and closed his door.

Every fiber of my being screamed for me to ask him, ask him! Was it confirmed I was going to go see Mom? Please say yes. Was it? However, I did not. I could not. My place as a child forbade such intrusion into the adult world. Even if the matter was related to me.

We rode to the airport in silence. When we arrived, I could barely see anything but the two-story white building with a glass tower. When we reached the public parking in the front of the loading area, then and only then did I allow myself to cry, but by then, I was crying because of something different. By then, I had understood that though I may have gained my mother, I had lost the only family I had ever known. I looked up at my uncle; he looked down at me earnestly for the first time. He told me to behave, care for myself, and know that the spirits would always watch after me. I positioned myself there crying, unable to say anything, just affirming to him that I would not be a disappointment.

Car to the loading area, loading area to the plane. A woman in a blue vest took me and sat me down next to a window somewhere down the left aisle. She attached a strap over my legs to keep me from moving too much. Not that I was going anywhere—by this time, I was so terrified I thought I would pee myself. I kept tugging at my dress and looking at the perfectly calm older man sitting next to me in the dark grey suit. He seemed strangely familiar with his closely shaven head and glasses, reading the newspaper. But as hard as I tried, I could not remember ever seeing him.

Then I looked outside the small oval-shaped window at people. Everyone was going on so casually about his or her business. Some were pushing the cart or carrying luggage, and everyone seemed so peaceful from my left to right. I wondered why no one knew how terrified the little girl in the plane's window seat was. As my fear grew, the man beside me looked over and told me to relax in Creole, "You will be fine," he said. I nodded yes, as I remained to stare down at my interlocked fingers, knowing damn well there was no way I was calming down.

A few minutes later, the woman in the blue vest came by to ensure I remained seated correctly. I replied I was okay, and she went away again. A little while later, the plane took off, along with the contents of my stomach.

The terminal at the end of our trip was bright. Like the fundamental tunnel passageway, we are told to expect on our journey from this world to the next. I wonder if that is how it felt to die. After all, I had just left one life for another. I stood there stunned by all the activity, all the noise, and all the words being spoken in languages I never knew existed, amazed by sight. The flight attendant from the plane took my hand and brought me to a counter where a white American was waiting. It was the first time I had seen someone of that complexion outside of television. Marie told me to stay there, and she walked away. The eyes of the American followed Marie. I turned around just in time to see the man from the plane seated next to me, dressed in a dark suit, handing her an envelope as he walked away in the opposite direction. I caught her eye for a minute, and hope surged within me that she would return to my side since she was the only person I knew. However, she only winked at me and went in the opposite direction. My heart sank.

As I turned around to face the gentleman before me. I felt panic build inside me again. He looked at me oddly, with a smile that didn't seem real. He kept asking me a question I could not understand. The only word I knew was *"passport."* So, I handed him my passport as my uncle had instructed and remained mute, hoping that some action might resolve whatever problem he was having with me, but it did not. He kept asking me repeatedly, who was picking me up? But I didn't speak English, didn't know what he was saying, and could not answer.

I was on the verge of tears when my mother arrived at the receiving counter and took charge of me from the now-concerned man. She came in like the sun breaking apart the clouds after a storm. I did not really remember what she looked like, but as soon as she walked in, I knew she was my mother, or at least I hoped she was. She was beautiful and smelled so good as she glided to stand beside me. They spoke, and he smiled and gave her my papers. She handed him a white envelope. She grabbed my hand and gently tugged me to follow.

I didn't cry when I saw her. I did not even speak. Instead, I stared at her, her hand holding mine, and realized that her caramel skin was darker than mine, yet it glistened like gold under the florescent light, setting aglow her light brown hair that fell down past her shoulders onto an aqua top and dark blue skirt. She was speaking to me, and I was somehow answering her, though I am not sure I ever really heard the questions. She is so beautiful, was the only thought running through my mind, even prettier than those French women on TV. I hoped without really knowing that I somehow looked like her.

We stopped just long enough for her to have a general examination of my arms and legs. Then, she asked me if I was hungry and said something about how skinny I was.

"You were not my first choice to bring up here," she said. "I wanted to bring your sister Maggie first because she was younger, but Anderson, your stepfather, said it would be better if we brought you before you got too old."

I nodded yes to all her statements, not understanding what they meant at the time. Then, finally, she grabbed the one satchel I carried with me, which contained my life's possessions at the age of nine, and led me out of the airport terminal of Miami International.

Now I sat, nearly 300 miles away from the city I called home, reminiscing on what seemed like an event from a half-dozen lifetimes ago. Staring at a multi-color pipe screen saver on a computer desktop, wondering what had happened to me.

In my earlier years, I did not take shit from people. I would have gotten into one fight with Michael, and if it resulted in disrespect, I would have walked away from him, never looking back. Now here I was after countless incidents of him having no regard for my feelings, secretly wishing that things would work out with him. That was crazy.

I had only been sixteen when the death of Mrs. J opened my eyes to the reality that not everybody we thought we loved, loved us. And although my mother had spent the years between me getting off that plane and finally leaving her house pounding into me through actions and words, that relationships were for mutual financial benefit only and nothing else. Yet, I still believed in love, even though I was unsure what love was or how one got it. I still felt in it.

The only thing my mother had done by her repeatedly lecturing me on the cause and effect of relationships was equip me with the mentality to approach every new relationship with a surgeon's precision on the operating table.

I would love it with all my heart and wanted everything to go perfectly, but I proceeded cautiously, constantly wary of any mistreatment someone might cause me.

Did love actually exist? Yes, but my experiences had taught me that I was not supposed to go out of my way or lose myself trying to find it. If it was meant to happen, then it would. That was my answer when I was younger and perhaps more competent for anyone who would have dared ask about my stance. But, of course, I would have never taken Michael back or believed in his lies. Instead, after an early life of instability and fear, I had tried to control the only thing I knew no one could take from me or use against me—myself.

I often watch my boy-crazy friends at sixteen, wondering why they would forgive a man who cheated on them or treated them like shit.

Therefore, it was with wonder that I looked at myself in the reflection of the computer screen. And wondered what had happened to change my position on the subject. When had I started acting like those friends I used to look at and shake my head in disapproval?

I remained there for a moment. The ducks were quacking, birds were singing, and the sun shone brightly. Everything was right with the world beyond this room. It was only my internal world falling apart. Let my thoughts fester on that idea. Everything was all right with the world, and it was just me who was falling apart.

I knew my thoughts were beginning to wander onto a path of denigration. But I let it go there. I needed to do this to endure and bury myself in a world of cynicism. I had learned early in life to disbelieve in the world and whomever I thought was responsible for me being in this state, even if it meant blaming myself for having forgotten those lessons. I needed to find the anger inside the pain so I could have the strength to deal.

What most people don't understand about life and adversity is that it is not the mistakes you make that define you as a person. Everybody makes mistakes—how you proceed with your life after those mistakes make you stronger. I had spent so much time being one of those women who walked through life proud to be the modern feminist. The ones who believed they didn't need a man just wanted one to share their life with. What about sex? That's what toys are for—the batteries last longer. What about having a baby? Two words for you—artificial insemination. You need a man to protect you. We would not need protection if it weren't for the men on this earth.

I had heard all their reasoning before and theories on why women needed men. When I had decided to pit my intellect against one of theirs on so many occasions. I had always conquered all their arguments. I knew I did not need a man, but I wanted one. I wanted a Prince Charming to bring flowers and tell me how pretty I was every day.

I pushed away from the screen, closing my eyes as I tilted my head back. My thoughts were becoming a whirlpool of past memories and present situations. I remember how I used to watch *The Little Mermaid* and think how like her I was. I was different from everybody in my family because of my looks, a parent who didn't understand me, and friends who wanted me to change. Disney movies had been my escape from the actuality of my life. Now I wondered if all those fairytale movies had finally gotten to me. Were the fairytales of princes rescuing the princesses and loving them forever implanted in my subconscious, and had I gone into every relationship wishing that the person I was with were my prince? Had I turned into Mrs. J along the way, blinding myself to the truth, hoping that what I felt was love?

I stood and began to walk to the kitchen while making a mental note to sue those fat corporate pigs at Disney for ruining my romantic expectations of men. But, hey, if people can sue McDonald's for being overweight, I could undoubtedly sue Mickey for my relationship problems, if not my mental ones.

Unexpectedly, a hint of truth came into my mind as I went to the kitchen. Maybe the reason why I cried at the end of my relationships when I was younger had nothing to do with love. But I had simply wished that the discovery of love was as simple as a two-hour cartoon or movie, as we had been trained to expect through books, movies, songs, and every other manufactured fairytale.

Sure, every woman wanted to think that at the beginning of every new relationship, something special would come from it. But had I slowly changed who I was, thinking that my new self would be more deserving of a Prince Charming since my old self had been nothing more than a white roach? Consciously, I knew who I was, or I thought I did. But subconsciously, I did not. I don't suppose anyone really knows themselves deep down.

But what happens when those two parts of yourself collide? Is the result an unwitting melding of two characters into one mind with only one knowledge? Did that new mental union contain a balance, or was one personality more dominating than the other? Moreover, what if the new dominating consciousness was the more passive you, and you had unwillingly changed yourself into a more submissive individual? Now you start to accept mistreatment as the norm when typically, you have always thought of yourself as someone who would have never stood for this behavior.

Okay, let us say for a minute that this combining of my conscious and subconscious mental state did happen. And for all rationale, let's also say that I was walking around talking a good game of my strength and resolve to slowly turn into a cream puff.

Indeed, I hadn't just woken up one day and decided, hey, this guy may be the best I will ever get, so let's deal with all his narcissistic bullshit, so he won't leave me.

No. Like all things. There was a beginning. If there was a beginning. There was a middle and, hopefully, an end. So, I opened the refrigerator door, took out a

Corona, and looked through the utensil drawer until I found a bottle opener. Checking my watch. It was ten-thirty in the morning. "Fuck it—it's five o'clock somewhere."

I returned to the black leather sofa across from the 57" Toshiba. The spot where Michael sat earlier was no longer warm from his body heat but instead had turned as cold as his attitude toward me. I stayed there for a minute, not really watching TV, just sort of spacing, troubled by the problems of my present circumstance.

The same two questions kept repeating in my head. When did having love become so important in my life? And how did I become so obsessed with making my relationships work that I started letting assholes run my life?

The questions themselves were simple enough. It was the answers that were cryptic.

Taking the final gulp of the beer from the bottle, I exhaled deeply, hoping to release some negative energy just as

Prince Charming walked through the door. He looked at me. I looked at him. He glared at the bottle, and I said nothing. Finally, I got up to throw it away.

"Even alcoholics would call this early for a drink." He locked the door behind him

"Fuck off, Michael. I'm not your dad," I muttered as I caught the Walgreens bag he tossed over the wooden counter separating the kitchen from the living room. He continued without breaking his stride to the patio, neither looking back at me nor replying to my comment. I stood there for a minute, frozen under the fluorescent light, the bag clinched in my hand.

Breathe, I reminded myself. Just breathe. The good Lord would never allow such a catastrophe as my pregnancy to be part of this drama already in. progress.

Chapter IX

It is always darkest before dawn...

It seemed like I had spent hours in front of the television. The remote was in my right hand, flipping through channels robotically, independent of my mind's wandering thoughts. The glass of water was already half-empty, not to mention the beer I had already had this morning. Yet, still, after all that, it seemed like my bladder was not responding for fear of the results.

Michael was outside on the porch smoking another cigarette and talking to someone on the phone. Who? I had no idea.

The E.P.T. test was out of the box, staying safe and cleanly wrapped in its foil packet on top of it. From time to time, I cast a sideways glance at it. The view seemed to be magnetized from an angle. This was not the first time I had to do this, but I swore it would be the last. This time it scared the shit out of me, and fear is a great motivator. Finally, he poked his head through the glass door. The white horizontal blinds on top were propelled forward by force and then came back to their resting position against the glass with a click.

"Can you go yet?" he asked, not even bothering to hear my answer before he docked right back out the door to take a drag off the cigarette. My mouth was half-open to answer him, but I closed it and swallowed my unspoken words.

The wall clock ticked on, with each second stretching to infinity. Then, finally, a crane's call broke through the sounds of the outside wildlife.

Flip. CNN—eighty dead due to a suicide bomber in Afghanistan. Flip. CNBC— the United States deficit has reached a record high again. Flip. Man kills his pregnant wife and unborn child...

If the human species was being watched by other beings, we were a great model of cruelty and hate.

It had only been one minute since Michael had closed the door on me, and I finally felt the urge to grab the foil packet and run to the bathroom to piss out my future, so to speak. But, instead, I left the teddy bear I had squeezed tipped over on the couch, probably relieved to be free from the pressure I had inflicted on its small stuffed body.

The instructions were simple enough, and the company manufacturing the test was so caring that they even had them in Spanish. So, there I sat and waited, leaving the little white stick with its tiny purple writing lying next to the bathroom sink like some fortune teller's crystal ball, waiting to reveal my future.

God, please do not let me be pregnant. Father, I pray to you, don't let this happen to me. I prayed before exiting the white chrome-decorated bathroom

I went back to sitting in front of the TV. The remote was no longer in my hand. My eyes were closed, and I was praying, begging desperately for a miraculous cure to what ailed me. Dazed and scared, but sure that I could not be pregnant; God in all his wisdom could not find anything positive in adding a baby to my present situation, could He?

"Did you take the test yet?" The excellent draft that accompanied Michael through the door stirred me more than his words. Of course, by now, I was as emotionally empty as that Corona bottle in the trash was devoid of alcohol, except the bottle probably felt better about itself.

"Yes, it's ..." I didn't get to finish my thought as he rushed in from the patio, around the couch, and into the bathroom, moving so fast through the small room that he sent the Lazy Boy into a half-turn.

I turned to face the entrance to the hall where the bathroom was. I heard the snap; Michael made a sound by pressing his forefinger and thumb together. The punctuation at the end of the thought emphasized the occurrence. I wish I knew what the hell it meant.

"It's not time yet. Whatever it says, the instructions were for at least another minute's worth of waiting time," I blurted out too quickly, hoping that speaking those words would keep Michael from revealing whatever was in his hand.

"It didn't need the extra time." He walked out of the bathroom to face me. I did nothing. He did not have to say it. Michael's demeanor was worth a thousand words.

"It's positive."

I think of myself as a writer, a pretty good one, at least, I hope. I have searched Oxford, Webster, Google, the encyclopedia, and even the Bible, and let me tell you one thing I have learned after all that research. No words that have ever been written in English, or any other language, can adequately describe the chaos of emotions a woman feels when presented with that kind of news, especially in my current situation. Therefore, I will not try to.

I looked up at Michael. He looked like someone had just told him his grandmother had taken him out of her Will. His usually well-tanned complexion was ash gray. I do not think that accidentally answering a door that death was knocking on would cause his skin to drain to such an ugly hue.

I burst into tears and ran. Michael's reflexes were good. He reached out to restrain me, but my terror was greater. I was through the door and down three flights of stairs before I knew where I was going. I ran, moving faster than I should have been, hoping that if I ran quickly enough, I would gain Superman speed and return in time. However, it did not happen. What did happen was I plunged down the last flight of stairs, not looking where I was going. I miss-stepped, stumbled forward, tripped on a tree root, and fell face-first into the grass by the lake. Dirt filled my mouth. The force of the impact cut open the palm of my hand and scraped my knees as I landed. I lay in the grass, bruised, sore, and crying. Nothing like the goddess I prided myself on being.

Lying there in the grass. I must have seemed like some overgrown child. That had been picked on by a group of bullying kids in school. I lay there and prayed for spontaneous combustion, for death, for any catastrophic incidents to happen so that this latest problem in my now mounting list of fuck-ups could automatically be resolved.

Nothing is ever resolved by death, and God tells me that every time he ignores my pleas for execution. However, as the daylight shined, the birds sang, and the wind blew, I felt God had forsaken me and that nature reminded me, "You mean nothing in the greater scheme of things." As I contemplated my uselessness, a shadow fell over my face. The light outlined it, hugging it. Michael's form emerged into my line of sight, blocking out the shine. Stooping down, he helped me up to my feet, gently wiping away the dirt on my face as he picked a blade of grass out of my hair and wrapped his arms around my waist. I stood as distant from him as his hold on me would allow, tears running down my soiled face. Finally, he pulled me close and let me cry on his shoulder. We stayed there under the sober warmth of the sun. I took comfort in what was the source of my pain, Michael being kind enough to provide it.

The breeze that caressed us smelled faintly of pine. But then, time stood still for a minute, and the pain I felt was overcome by love or at least a good imitation of it. It was one of the few times in the past two weeks that we had shown each other affection. Sex did not count.

As I stood there consoling myself in his arms, I wished I could somehow relate to myself what I knew our future would be like, knowing damn well we would not get better. Michael walked me up the stairs and into the apartment the whole time, his arms never leaving my waist. We sat on the couch, a torrent of tears running down my face. He kept a hold of me, letting me cry on him. It reminded me of the first time Michael had been a shoulder for me to cry.

More than two years ago, Daniel had inadvertently confessed to his affair. What made it worse was that I had known the girl. She had been an associate of mine and an old friend of his. I have learned it is always worse when you see a woman. Sam used to come over to our apartment to eat. We used to go to the beach together and go out to the club together. We were a little crew; I had been so dull-witted to be comforted knowing Daniel was *not* attracted to her. Daniel acted as if he didn't even like me being associated with Sam, even though she was more his friend than mine. However, I consoled him on his worries. Letting him know I would not let her negatively influence me with the drugs she took and that I just wanted part of his circle of friends, which, now to think of it, was ironically funny.

How it all happened is how the story always seems to play out. Daniel and I argued about my new job and time there one night. That night he stormed out of the apartment, slamming the door on his way out. I called him and discovered he had gone to a party to blow off steam. So, I left it at that. When he did not come home that night, I figured he had gotten too drunk to drive home.

I knew I was bullshitting myself. No matter how drunk Daniel got, no one could ever make him realize driving was not something he should do.

That night after many glasses of Merlot and calling him an infinite number of times without success, I finally fell asleep alone. The following day I went to work thinking when I got home, he and his boy Ian would be there, and we would act like we never fought, drink some more and move on.

About eleven o'clock that morning, Ian called me.

"I woke up from sleeping off last night's partying and wanted to know if Danny made it home okay. I tried to call him, but he was not answering his phone. So, I figured I would call you since he's probably still sleeping after all the Rum he downed last night,"

I felt like the wind had been knocked out of me. With a tremble in my voice, I said.

"Daniel hadn't come home. I tried calling him, but it just kept going to voicemail. Oh God, Ian, what if something happened to him all because we got into s stupid fight about my job, Jesus." I said as I started to feel a shiver of fear running down my spine. "If he was too drunk to drive, why didn't you hide his keys? Why didn't you make him stay by you?" I screamed through the receiver.

"But Selene, he didn't leave alone. I would not have let him. Calm down. I'm sure his okay. You know him, he had too much to drink. So, he probably passed just out somewhere," he finished

"Who did he leave with, Ian? I continued yelling.

The question, it seemed, was not something he had been prepared to answer.

He started with, "I am not too sure."

Then,

"He's okay. Let me find him."

Now I knew there was something he was not comfortable telling me, and I was not letting him off the phone until he told me. After a minute of dead air between us, Ian finally gave in and answered.

"Sam, Danny told everyone at the party he would give her a ride home."

"Sam, okay, that's not a problem. I'll call her and see if he is okay."

"Selene, I don't think you should call her. I think you should let him call you back" There was something in Ian's voice that said there was something more, something he was holding back.

"Why?" I asked

"Daniel was really pissed last night. He got really drunk. Just let him call you, okay?"

"Okay," I said with no real intention of holding true to my word.

I would ask him why he didn't want to call, but I didn't push. After all, it was only Sam. I had nothing to worry about when it came to her. I mean, I didn't trust her. I've had friends that had slept with my boyfriend before, but I trusted him. I was sure there was another explanation for what appeared to be happening in my relationship at that moment.

I hung up with Ian and called Daniel, but there was no answer. My fear had reached the peak of its climax. First, I called his mom, thinking he was still mad at me, which was why he was not answering. She had not heard from him either. Next, I called his grandmother with the same result. I was becoming frantic. I kept twisting the diamond ring on my left hand, thinking that if something had happened with the person who owned my heart, I would know, surely there would be a sign. I hated when he got so drunk that he needed a driver, but nobody could stop him.

He was six-feet-four inches tall and two-hundred and twenty pounds with a Puerto Rican attitude to boot. His friends had found out the hard way that getting his keys away from him was like fighting with a wild boar. Ultimately, the boar would be fine, but they would have serious injuries. Knowing that sitting in the sales office was not accomplishing anything, I should get my ass on the sales floor before my manager came looking for me. I decided to try again to reach him on his phone, too scared not to, even though I was putting my job on the line. Danny was more important.

When he finally answered his cell, I could tell by his voice that I had just woken him up. He must have accidentally hit the speakerphone button on his phone because I could clearly hear a kiss. Then Daniel said,

"What the fuck?"—as if in surprise.

Then the phone dropped, or at least that is what I hoped happened. But unfortunately, it was too late when Daniel picked up the phone from wherever it had landed. I had already heard her screaming in the background at the top of her lungs.

"Fuck you, Daniel. Don't act like you didn't enjoy last night. You weren't thinking about that bitch when your face was buried inside my pussy."

He hastily picked up the phone and hung it up. I called him back, chasing after my own poison. He picked up.

"Babe, I am so sorry," he said.

My world shattered at those five words. Never would I have believed that Daniel was capable of cheating on me. I didn't let him finish. I hung up the phone and threw it against the opposite wall. Sitting at my desk in the sales office, I felt alone, crying into my monthly planner.

Michael walked in as boisterous as ever a few minutes later. Apparently looking for me because our manager wanted the only saleswoman he had on the sales floor to rub the fact that he had just completed the first sales of the day in my face.

When he found me at my desk crying, he did not ask what was wrong. He knew Daniel, and I had trouble. Everybody did, and he figured a severe problem must have happened between us when he saw the ring on my desk instead of on my hand. He walked across the room and picked up my phone. The battery had come apart from the actual cell phone. Michael put it back together and put it in front of me, and without saying a word, Michael helped me to my feet and held me. It seemed like we were standing there for hours.

"It's going to be okay," He whispered in my ear, his warm breath caressing my neck. "Selene, we all know he's not in the same league as you. You could and will do much better than Daniel".

He continued with things I already knew but felt better hearing from somebody else. So that afternoon, Michael snuck me out of the dealership, where we worked through the service bay. When we finally reached his car, he called our manager from his cell and told him I was not feeling good and that he was using his lunch to take me home.

I did not want to go home. I could not face Danny yet, and I knew Danny was on his way there to try to explain to me. However, what could he explain? How could he explain it to me? Just the thought made me start crying harder. I wanted to break that asshole's neck and then castrate him. I told all this to Michael as he helped me into his car. Michael thought castration was a bit extreme, even if he deserved it. Therefore, he suggested we go to his place, twenty minutes from the dealership. We would just chill until I felt okay enough to go home. That Saturday, more than two years ago, we had sat on this same couch with him, letting me cry against the seat's armrest until I finally fell asleep with a slight headache and an incurable heartache.

He left me there sleeping, covered me with a blanket and left a note to make myself at home, and went back to work. When Michael returned home, Daniel had left me many messages; the voicemail box on my phone was full. Finally, I felt less distraught and asked Michael to take me to my car. He obliged.

Michael had been outstanding. I had been as thankful to him for coming to my rescue then as I do now, even though he was part of the problem.

I lifted my head to face him.

"It wasn't time to check the test yet. The test said three to five minutes for an accurate result. You looked too soon," I said, as if that statement alone would change the result.

"Baby girl." Michael took a deep breath.

I took all these little signs of his personality in. His calm demeanor and aloofness to the situation made it as if he had been prepared to handle this.

"It's not a mistake, or at least not when it's a positive reading. It could only be wrong if it had been said. negative." He was so sure, so knowledgeable as if he had been through this a hundred times before.

Later, I would find out he had been, at least twice, if not a hundred times. I would never have found out if I had not found myself in the same problem with Mr. Smith as his previous girlfriends. However, feeling ignorant, scared, and hateful, I only listened, watched, and cried. Turning away from him, I stood wiping away tears on my blue low-rise jeans. He tried to restrain me. I twisted my wrist out of his hand, walked around the couch, and into the bathroom. With trembling hands, I picked up the test. Two clearly defined pink lines stared back at me, one in the square window and one in the oval. Positive. There was no doubt even if I didn't believe Michael. My eyes were not deceiving me.

The stick fell from my hand into the sink. My body doubled over, and I threw up all over the toilet. The acidic smell filled my nose, causing me to gag and vomit even more. It took maybe five minutes for my stomach to empty itself of water and beer until all left were painful dry heaves.

I flushed the toilet, wiped the seat and all the other contaminated surfaces with toilet paper, and flushed it again. While washing my face in the sink, I stopped to look at myself in the mirror. My nose was pinkish from crying, my lips red from biting into them, and my whole face was swollen. However, my eyes, dark brown, so narrowly shaped at the corners I could have passed for Asian, typically beautiful, told the sad story of what I was going through. I looked away, too ashamed to face myself. When I returned from the bathroom, Michael was back on the porch.

I could see him sitting on one of the suede patios chairs through the slants in the horizontal blinds on the door. The vast yellow phone directory lay on his lap, cigarette in one hand, cell phone in the other. He was deep in a conversation with someone. I remained there for a minute, wondering with whom and how deep the discussion could be since I had only been in the bathroom for ten, maybe fifteen minutes. Then, opening the door, I walked outside.

"Thank you, Stacey. We'll definitely get back in touch with you." He looked up long enough to see me standing there and hung up the phone.

"Hey, you, okay? Do you want some water or anything?"

He began to stand to help me sit. I motioned for him to remain sitting.

"No, I'm fine."

Tiny pulses of anger had begun to reverberate through me. An awful feeling in the pit of my stomach started to develop about what Mike was doing out here with the yellow pages so soon after a positive pregnancy test. I could clearly see what page the phone book was opened to, yet I asked anyway.

"Who was that?"

Coolly, he took a drag from the cigarette and placed the phone beside the mosaic patio table.

"Oh, her ... she's just a nurse or something from a women's center."

He slowly looked up at me as he spoke those words. There was a hint of anxiety in his persona, but he managed to control it. A cool breeze blew around us, caressing my face and barely moving small strands of his gelled mane.

I took a deep breath and stared back at him. Tears threatened to reclaim me, but I fought them off.

"What type of women's center, Michael?" I finally managed to get out without losing my resolve.

"Oh, Selene, sit down, please. We need to talk."

He had begun to rise up to help me sit beside him, but I took a step back reflexively. Now my hands were balled into tight little fists. I glared at him, and he sat back down. He took another drag off the cigarette. I never realized how much I hated that putrid nicotine-filled scent until now.

"What kind of center?" I snarled at him through gritted teeth.

"You couldn't have possibly thought we could keep it," he spat out as he flicked the butt off the patio and onto the parking lot beneath.

For a moment, the world slowed to a pace a snail could keep up with. Then, my body began to move of its own accord as my mind wrapped around the gall of the bastard. I took the three steps that remained between us in one swift stride. The wind raised its voice in sympathy to my disgust about the insult Mike had just imparted upon me. I stopped in front of him, and as my whole body trembled with rage, I slapped the shit out of him. The sound of my palm across his left cheek echoed off the wings of the wind. And flew out across the parking lot underneath the balcony.

"How dare you make that decision for me. You, you asshole!"

Although my actions were stunning, I felt due justification for them as I turned and walked away.

Michael stayed there bewildered for a few seconds. Never had there ever been any type of physical confrontation between us. Truth be told, I was so surprised at myself. I almost tripped over one of the chairs, retreating into the apartment. Having regained his composure, he stood up and reached for me, but I got to the door before he caught me. Stepping into the apartment backward, I yanked the door shut in front of me while simultaneously engaging the deadbolt. Unfortunately, he pulled it open a fraction too late.

"Selene dammit. Open the door. Selene!"

I kept walking. How could I have been so stupid? I thought.

I had moved more than 300 miles to be with him.

I walked over to the counter. Michael was now banging on the door, begging me to be reasonable.

Ha! Reasonable.

I slipped on my sandals.

I had left all my friends, family, and life for him!

I grabbed my keys.

Bang, bang, bang!

I gave it all up and moved here because I wanted to believe in him, believe in him, and feel what? That love could somehow actually exist between us.

But that was a lie. I had known better. I had only been lying to myself about my happiness with Michael. Hoping that things between us could be more than what they were and that hope had only been a desperate lover's dreams. A dream I could somehow influence and therefore make things better. Isn't that the dream that we could find a person we care for and turn all his negative traits into positive ones?

Or is the dream that the person is perfect to start with? But unfortunately, there are no such things as perfect people, and you cannot change a person for the better. People will have to want to change. We always know when we are in an irresolvable situation, yet we just lie to ourselves, hoping . . .

Hoping what?

This time is different from all the other times. I picked up my purse and cell and walked out of the front door, with Michael still trapped on the patio.

Men Are Not The Problem

Continues in –

Volume II

About the author

Luna Charles, is a Haitian-American writer who has authored numerous books, articles, and essays. Besides being an accomplished author, Luna is also a dedicated student of Theology, Metaphysics, and Philosophy. As a mother of two lovely girls, Luna has spent most of her life in South Florida.